Milwaukee

BERNICE RUBENS

Milwaukee

LITTLE, BROWN AND COMPANY

A *Little, Brown* Book

First published in Great Britain
by Little, Brown and Company in 2001

A CIP catalogue record for this book
is available from the British Library.

ISBN 0 316 85571 5

Typeset in Galliard by M Rules
Printed and bound in Great Britain
by Clays Ltd, St Ives plc

Little, Brown and Company (UK)
Brettenham House
Lancaster Place
London WC2E 7EN

For Parvin and Michael Laurence

Milwaukee

What does one pack for dying? Annie wondered. She'd packed often enough in her time. For cruising, well almost, but one mustn't think about that, for dancing, for swimming. But for dying?

What would she not be seen dead in? But what did it matter any more. Some nighties would do, and a frock, until bedbound. She folded them into the holdall, and called to Clemmie that she was ready.

Clemmie, her life-long friend, was waiting to drive her there. Not a word passed between them, only the gear change breaking the silence. Until they arrived at the hospice gates, and Annie began to laugh. Then Clemmie joined her. It was the worst way, and the best, to express their despair.

It was more of a hotel than a hospice, though its purpose was to be a bit of both. If you didn't 'go gentle into that good night', then at least they made sure that you would go in luxury.

'They' being the staff, a kindly group, more used to the dying than the quick, well-versed in the language of denial when that was called for, or of resignation if that were the required code.

Matron showed them to Annie's room. There were no stairs to climb. The entire building was spread out on one floor. The room was more of a cubicle, curtain-screened from the next, but large enough to house a small wardrobe, a chest of drawers, a table, and a bookshelf full of books. Annie scanned the titles and from them learnt the disposition of the previous occupant. They were mainly books of short stories, an acknowledgement of limited time. A dip-into Bible was part of the small library, an apt collection for such a place, and Annie was pleased with it.

Clemmie unzipped the holdall. 'Shall we unpack?' she asked. She was including herself in Annie's last journey and would travel with her to the end.

'Wait a little,' Annie said. To unpack was to resign and was to exclude any possibility of going home.

'Just the nightdress,' Clemmie said. It seemed less final.

'Let's see what the lounge is like,' Annie said. 'I'll do it later.'

They walked arm-in-arm down the long corridor to the draw-ing room at its end. The room was full of flowers and smelt like a funeral parlour. But there were easy chairs and loungers, and landscape pictures on the wall. Through the window a splendid spread of cherry-blossom heralded the arrival of spring and, at this sight, Annie's heart lifted and for a moment she forgot where she was and why. A nurse followed them into the room and effected the introductions. Mrs Withers saved her the trou-ble and on her own account introduced herself.

'I'm Mrs Withers,' she said. '*Mrs* Withers,' she stressed, as if that title saved her from a life of total failure. She put down her knitting-needles and offered her hand. Annie took it and wondered what she was knitting. It looked like a shapeless scarf. The ball of wool was clearly running out and the sight of its limited term depressed her.

'Miss Hopkins,' the nurse moved towards Mrs Withers' neighbour.

'Jane,' Miss Hopkins said, and offered a wan smile. She was young, in her thirties perhaps, and frail. With a trembling hand she was painting her nails, as heart-warming a sight as the cherry-blossom.

Mrs Locke was next on the list. She looked very old. Yet she rose from her seat to take Annie's hand and to assure her that she would be happy in her new home. The word 'home' unsettled Annie a little, but she managed a smile. Mrs Locke had no illusions. She knew that she was 'home' and certain in any conscious state never to leave it.

A few more introductions followed. Some were welcoming but others indifferent, even hostile to invasion. A newcomer could be a disturbance, either to their own resignation or to their own denial. Each attitude required its own routine, a routine that was stubbornly closed to any alternative, and a new arrival threatened to suggest other possibilities. 'I'm here to mind my own business,' Annie wanted to tell them, though she wasn't quite sure what that business was. But she knew that she would have to learn.

It was time for Clemmie to leave. 'I'll be back tomorrow,' she said, kissing her friend on the cheek. Annie embraced her in her turn.

'Come, sit by me.' Mrs Withers pointed to an empty chair beside her, and though Annie would have wished to return to her room and face out the holdall on her bed, she felt it would be lacking in courtesy to refuse Mrs Withers' invitation.

'I'm here just for a rest,' she whispered to Annie. 'Simply for a rest,' she insisted. Death was something that happened to other people. Annie let it lie. Each to her own illusions, she thought. Then Mrs Withers happily launched into a recital of diagnoses of the residents. 'That lady over there,' she whispered, pointing to Miss Hopkins. 'She's only thirty-two. No hope for her, poor soul. She's got, you know what. Heard her crying out last night in her sleep. Looks terrible, doesn't she?' Mrs Withers said with some delight, and Annie caught her smiling into her knitting. She turned away, sickened, and looked again at the cherry-blossom for solace. And then at Miss Hopkins, who was flapping her hands so that the nail polish would dry. She would paint her own nails, she decided, though she had never done so in her whole life. Clemmie would show her how. She excused herself. 'I must unpack,' she told Mrs Withers though she had no intention of doing so, but she needed to be alone, if only to out-face her holdall.

She sat on her bed and stared at it, and she had a feeling that she had been in this place for a long time, yet it was only a few days ago that her life had so radically changed.

First, the news of Freddie's death. She had not been well for some time, and Clemmie had brought her her breakfast in bed. Though she had no appetite. Not even to read the morning paper, which Clemmie laid on the bedspread. But she could not avoid the headline. It stared at her from off the front page. FREDDIE MORGAN DIES, she read. Clemmie seized the paper, cursing herself for not having noticed the news that would break her friend's heart. But Annie had simply raised an eyebrow. The movement had nothing to do with surprise. Nor with sorrow. But she knew that if he had died fifty or so years ago, her mourning would have been life-long. But fifty years ago, Freddie didn't die. Instead he asked Annie to marry him. That was a lifetime past, and in the end nothing mattered. Nothing registered. Not enough grief.

She read the headline again. 'Oh,' she said. Not even an exclamation mark was audible, let alone shock or sorrow. Just a simple monosyllabic acceptance. Then she had fingered her night-shawl, comforted by the knowledge that as one grew older one was less threatened by feelings. But over the years she had sunk into a languid limbo, safe from recall or nostalgia. She pushed the breakfast tray aside and sank back into the pillows.

'The doctor will be here soon,' Clemmie said. 'He will have the test results.' She had rouged Annie's cheeks and primped her hair, though she knew that no beautifying could hide her friend's condition.

The doctor had not beaten about the bush. 'Nothing can be done, Annie,' he had said. 'It has gone too far. The tests have confirmed it.'

'But I feel well enough,' she had protested.

He had put his hand gently on her arm. He knew that she was choking on the question she was afraid to ask. 'About two months,' he had said. It was then, after so many limbo years of stifled feelings, that Annie had blown. Or rather the *feelings* had blown. They refused any longer to go back where they came from, that dark, forbidden no-man's land, and they exploded with rage. There was absolutely no justice in the doctor's verdict. After all her struggles, all her heartaches, was she not entitled to a time of peace that had nothing to do with the shroud? 'It's not fair,' she had screamed to herself and she found her rage invigorating. She was glad of it, and she would nurture it. It would be a weapon for survival.

There was no one at home capable of full-time care, so they

booked her into the hospice, where her dying would be painless and even, drug-conned, with the occasional glimpse of heaven. And that had been only yesterday. Yet she had held on to her rage, guarding it like a treasure, for it had detonated that limbo of indifference. It had prised open her stubborn mind, that mind that for so many years, afeared of response, of reaction, had refused recall, had dodged remembrance, had wiped the flashback clean. 'No more of that,' Annie said aloud. 'No more of that.' She unzipped the holdall with a certain relish. She had packed not for dying but for remembrance, for retrospection, and even for nostalgia.

She heard a bell and presumed it was a calling for lunch. She was astonished at her sudden appetite and she left her cubicle and sniffed her way to the dining room. Mrs Withers motioned her to the empty seat beside her. Annie would have preferred another's placing. She found Mrs Withers' death-delights faintly obscene. But she could not refuse the invitation. She had hardly settled herself when Mrs Withers pointed out the empty chair that should have housed Miss Hopkins.

'You missed the drama,' she said. 'Poor Miss Hopkins collapsed shortly after you left. Sank to the floor making the most blood-curdling noises, and still waving her hands so that the nail polish could dry. We won't be seeing her in the dining room any more.'

Although Annie understood Mrs Withers' closet despair, she found her an irritating companion. It was as if she was high on death and its paraphernalia, getting off on it, as it were, in ways unmentionable. Moreover, her constant Cassandra chatter was an intrusion into her own turbulent thoughts, those echoes from her past that she had to acknowledge, a disturbance of that hindsight journey that she must take, and even perhaps with occasional pleasure. She felt herself smiling and she wondered how a smile could form so easily after so many years of non-practice and neglect. Then she tested a laugh, so long untried, but that too had lost none of its skill. Mrs Withers heard the laugh as a pre-death delirium.

'Are you all right?' she asked, hopeful that a laugh was a herald of something that was nothing to laugh about.

'I'm perfectly all right,' Annie shouted to her. 'I have things to do, and "miles to go before I sleep". I shall die in my own good time, so you can save your orgasm, Mrs Withers, until I'm good and ready.'

That word, that long-forgotten word. It astonished her. It shipped her back into her girlhood, where such a word was comfortably at home. She felt as a young girl again, and nervous on the borders of recall. And with intrepid fear, she crossed the frontier. Fifty years ago. The golden years. And in those years, Freddie.

Annie was seventeen years old and in her last year at school. She stood at the front gates in her school uniform. And she took time to itemise it. After all, the doctor had given her two months. Time enough for detail and specification. Black, sensible lace-up shoes, the one shoestring too short for a bow which took some time to undo, until she couldn't be bothered and left it permanently unlaced. Then the black stockings, woollen and itchy, and the suspender belt that after its first wash never saw white again. The vest likewise, and the liberty-bodice, that quaint misnomer, the straitjacket of her childhood. The white blouse and permanently knotted tie and, over all, the black gymslip. At the thin leather belt, she hesitated. In it were six eyelets to accommodate whatever waist-measurement was applicable, and she noted that there was only one left for leeway. Then she trembled as she dared to think of her future.

The war was over. Sons and husbands were demobbed and the GIs went home. Amongst them, one from Wisconsin who'd scuttled back to Milwaukee and who'd carelessly left his seed behind. Just one collision it had taken, just one mindless moment in the back of a GI truck. Annie didn't know his name and she'd forgotten what he looked like, and little Mary, when she arrived, gave no clue. She resembled nobody.

All this Annie recollected without pain. So far, so palatable. But dare she now risk her father into her recall and the bitterness and pain that such a memory would evoke. So she was glad when she heard the breakfast bell. A reason to postpone. Her father could cool his heels outside the doors of her memory, and with luck and his natural impatience, he might even go away. But she knew it was no longer *his* doing that mattered. It was *her* recall, and to shut him out would be her own loss, her own denial. But first she would have her breakfast.

She walked down to the dining room and found herself seated yet again beside Mrs Withers.

'Good morning,' she said, biting into her toast. 'I hope you slept well. The first night in this place can be quite frightening. Especially on waking up when one realises where one is.'

Annie wished she had another placing. Two solid months of Mrs Withers was simply unfair. She was entitled to more genial company.

'I told you she was on the way out, didn't I,' Mrs Withers was saying.

'Who?' Annie asked.

'That poor girl, Miss Hopkins. Went in the night it seems.' She spread marmalade on her second piece of toast and Annie marvelled at the woman's appetite and she began to wonder whether Mrs Withers was indeed, as she claimed, not in this place to die but had wormed her way into the grounds which held such fertile soil for her *schadenfreude*. Annie hurried over her breakfast. She needed to be alone. She knew that her father still waited at the frontier of her recall, and fearfully she went to meet him, for anything was better than having to listen to Mrs Withers' miserable forebodings.

He had his back to the fire. A parson's stance, the only qualification for the clergy that he had managed to acquire. For he had failed all the others, and as a result he blamed God and he hated Him. Since he had been denied entry into the Church, he decided to better himself in un-Christian ways. This he did as a scrap-merchant, profiting dishonestly on every deal until he was very rich indeed. But he never forgave the Church and he stood with his back to the fire to spite it. He dabbled in other un-Christian ways. He enjoyed adultery for he knew that that would make the pulpit tremble. And he would happily have coveted his neighbour's ass, had his neighbour had one. In any case his neighbour was a homosexual and Annie's father thought he should be put down with all of his kind. Yet there had been a time when he had loved God and had been willing to serve Him all his life. But God had let him down. He'd let him fail his exams and that was proof enough that God didn't want him. He'd tried them a second time, giving God another chance, but again he failed. After that, not only did he cease to love God, be began to hate Him, and he sought out all manners and means to offend Him. But when it suited him, he still clung to some

time-honoured Christian values and he called them mightily
into service when he discovered his daughter's condition.

Annie had just come in from school. Her father, as usual, was
blocking the fire. She asked him to move so that she could repo-
sition a stool, and as she bent down to do so, her belt, now
precariously fixed on the last eyelet, broke its bonds, and as she
stood up her interesting condition could no longer be concealed.
Her gymslip draped like an ill-fitting smock. She cupped her hands
over her bulge and stood, terrified, waiting to be sentenced.

Her father stared at her, first at her face, as he gathered the
courage to lower his eyes to view the horror. He sniffed the
shame of it, the scandal, the disgrace; he sniffed it on behalf of
his friends and his neighbours, his golfing partners, especially
the latter on whom he depended for business.

'Mother,' he yelled. It sounded like a scream for help and
Annie's mother rushed in from the kitchen.

'What is it?' she said, but she saw what it was without being
told. She had thought that Annie was getting fat but now she
saw that it was not fat at all. It was a bulge of shame, of disgrace,
a what-will-we-tell-our-neighbours bulge, a what-have-we-
done-to-deserve-this bulge, and for a moment both of her
parents could have killed her.

Her father trembled, invaded by a sudden rush of Christian
fervour. 'Who's the father?' he yelled. He planned to force him
to the altar or to kill him.

Annie must have read his mind. 'He's in America,' she said.
'In Milwaukee.'

Then he feared the worst. In the course of his work he'd
come across several half-caste children, GI oversights. Some of
their sad grandfathers worked for him and he'd sympathised.
'Nigger, is he?' he shouted.

'What difference?' Annie had the courage to say, and she left the room. Let him stew, she decided. She would not afford him the relief of telling him the child would be white. She was appalled at his bigotry and he could jolly well suffer for it. She left the door ajar and stood behind it, eavesdropping. She felt she was entitled to hear her sentence.

'I'm not having her here,' she heard her father say. 'I'm not going to have my friends see her in that condition. God help me, but I've worked hard enough. I've got a position in this community. People respect me. What are they going to think that I've fathered such a slut? She's got to go.'

'What about university?' her mother dared.

'She's not going anywhere in that condition. She can forget university. It's her own fault. She's made her filthy bed. Now she can lie on it.'

Annie stifled her sobs. She wondered what flesh her father was made of, or indeed if it was flesh at all.

'We'll send her to Sheffield,' she heard him say. 'To Aunt Cassie. She'll take her. She'll have it there and get it adopted. And that will be the end of it. We'll say that Cassie is ill. She's gone to look after her.'

'But she's your daughter, your only child,' her mother dared to remind him.

'She's yours too,' her father shouted. 'The result of your loose upbringing.'

'I won't let her go,' her mother said.

Then her father whispered but the threat in his voice was ear-piercing. 'It's her or me,' he said. 'Make up your mind.'

Annie pressed her ear to the door. Her sentencing hung on her mother's choice. She waited. And all she heard was silence. It was the hardest blow, the most painful rejection of all. She remembered sinking to the floor then, and all was dark and silent.

As she recalled this incident, Annie wondered about its sequel. She must have spent some days in darkness and silence, days while arrangements were being made in whispers and shamefaced conspiracy. She recalled nothing more until she stood on the platform of Sheffield station, waiting for Aunt Cassie.

'There you are,' she heard a cheerful voice, and felt an embrace. Then the ride back to Aunt Cassie's house with no lecture and no recrimination. She remembered that she cried with gratitude.

'You're not to worry,' Aunt Cassie said. 'Everything will be seen to.' She wondered what 'seen to' meant and she feared her father's solution.

'I'm keeping it,' she said. 'I'm not giving it away.' She thought she'd better make that clear from the start, so that the business of adoption was not included in Aunt Cassie's 'seeing to'.

'If that's what you want,' Aunt Cassie said, 'then that's what you shall have.'

Aunt Cassie was her father's sister and they had never got on, and Annie wondered whether her aunt opposed the adoption in order to spite her brother. She knew that her father disapproved of Will, Aunt Cassie's husband. Whenever he referred to him, it was with contempt. For he was no more than a door-to-door salesman, with no ambitions to better himself. And his grammar was appalling. Cassie had never been invited to their house in their London suburb in case she brought Will with her and his illiteracy and rough manners would not impress her father's friends. Annie decided that she would love Will, whom she had

never met, even if he were unlikeable. But she had no trouble in
warming towards him. Uncle Will welcomed her as Aunt Cassie
had done, and Annie recalled her stay at their home with nothing but affection.

Uncle Will sold insurance. Door-to-door. When he didn't
feel like working, he stayed at home or tended his allotment.
There were always fresh vegetables in the house, and salads,
but little meat, and less fish. Yet the diet was healthy and Annie
blossomed. Pregnancy suited her. She carried with ease and
with pride. Will and Cassie did not favour secrets and she was
welcomed into their circle of friends without shame. She marvelled at the difference between her aunt's style of living and
that of her father. Poor as opposed to rich, informal other than
starch, regular pub knees-ups as opposed to stiff dinner-parties.
And finally happily married. For when she thought of her parents, their lives amounted only to manners and misery. She
thought about them less and less, but always with bitterness.
She would never forgive her father, which did not worry her, for
she knew that it would not worry *him*. But her mother was a
problem. Her father's rejection had not surprised her. It was in
character. But she was haunted by her mother's silence, the
silence of collusion. It was her mother's weakness that Annie
could not forgive, her cowardice. She had made no stand. When
faced with a choice between a bully and her daughter, her
option could not produce words. Yet she had chosen, and her
silence was her shame. She wondered whether her mother
would be by her side when the baby was born. But she doubted
it. Her father would forbid it, and her mother, in silence, would
stay at home.

Aunt Cassie had been appointed to deal with the adoption
procedures, and though she applied for the papers, and received

them, she did nothing about them, and appointments were ignored. She and Will were on Annie's side, and by the time Annie had but two weeks to her term, Cassie had already gathered most of the layette. Will was good with his hands and wood and he started to build a cradle, and the house throbbed with the joy of anticipation.

Until the phonecall. It was a Sunday. They were at the table. The three of them, playing gin rummy.

'Let it ring,' Will said. He had been dealt a good hand. 'It's Sunday. Can't be important.'

Aunt Cassie agreed. She suspected it was yet another call from her brother wanting a progress report on the adoption arrangements. So they let it ring. But it insisted for a long while.

'Somebody wants you very badly,' Annie said. 'Shall I answer it?'

'No. Leave it.' Will said.

The noise began to get on their nerves and each ring seemed to plead greater urgency. Then Cassie could stand it no longer. 'Bugger them,' she said, and she grabbed the phone with a furious 'Hello'. Annie and Will could hear the scream from the other end of the line. A woman's scream.

'Who is it?' Cassie yelled. 'And what's the matter?'

Will and Annie could hear no response, so they read Cassie's face for information.

'When?' Cassie whispered. 'And how?'

Then they saw a tear spurt from her eye and she began to sob uncontrollably.

Annie took the receiver from her hand. 'This is Annie,' she said. 'Who is it?'

'Your mother,' she heard. 'Your father's gone.'

'Where?' Annie asked.

'Dead, you stupid,' her mother said. 'Tell Cassie the funeral's on Friday. Two o'clock. St Andrew's Church. And you are not to come. D'you hear me?'

'I'll be there,' Annie said, and she banged the receiver back into its cradle.

Cassie had left the room.

'Leave her a bit,' Will said. 'She needs to be left alone. They wasn't very close, but a brother's a brother.' He took Annie's hand. 'You're entitled to go to your father's funeral,' he said. 'It's up to you.'

Annie wondered why she couldn't cry. She didn't even want to. She was too angry with her mother who, even now, free of his bigotry, still insisted upon it. She would go to the funeral, budding and close to flower, in order to spite her. To spite him too. And having done that, she might be able to forgive both of them.

The following day another patient died, so Mrs Withers happily informed her. A Mrs Foley whom Annie had never seen, since she had never appeared in the dining room. But Mrs Withers had visited her and had relished her slow decline. She embarked on a graphic description of that deterioration, but Annie excused herself, saying she had letters to write. But there were no letters to write. She simply had to go to her father's funeral.

They took an early morning train. The three of them. Will, who had never owned a suit, borrowed one from an undertaker friend, so he was suitably dressed for the occasion, though he was far from comfortable inside it. It gave the impression of deep mourning and he felt as if he were parading a lie for he was as indifferent to his brother-in-law's death as he had been to his life. Cassie tended to dress in black anyway, so her garb was appropriate. Annie had had to make do with a grey smock that Cassie had hurriedly run up on her sewing machine.

'Are we going straight to the church?' Annie asked.

'We'll be too early for that,' Cassie said. 'We'd better go to the house first. Then we can all go to the funeral together.'

'You know she told me not to come,' Annie said.

'Don't worry,' Cassie said. 'I'll deal with that when I get there.' She had little time for her sister-in-law, finding her a snob and uncaring. She hoped that sorrow might have mellowed her a little.

'How did he die?' Annie asked, for they had not spoken about it since the phonecall.

'Heart attack. On the golf course. Went out like a light, your mother said. Didn't feel a thing.'

Annie was comforted. It was enough that her father was dead. She wouldn't have wanted him to suffer.

Halfway to London, Will brought out the Thermos of tea and the box of sandwiches that he had made for the journey. They ate and drank with relish, trying to pretend that it wasn't a picnic. Even Cassie had cheered up a little. 'I'll feel better once I've seen him,' she said. 'You sort of want proof, don't you.' But Annie didn't care whether she saw him, boxed or not. Her father in the guise of a corpse was no less bigoted, no less vain, no less of a bully. She was not going to be conned by embalming cosmetics.

They took a taxi from the station. The driver had to be directed since he was not familiar with the area. Annie was nervous. She didn't know how her mother would receive her, and she misdirected the driver in order to postpone the meeting. In time, after much circling, they turned into Annie's street and she clutched at Will's hand to still her trembling.

'It'll all be all right,' he said to her, though he had no reason to think so. From Cassie's report, he knew that Mrs Dawson was a cold, unforgiving woman whom sorrow would not have mellowed. Indeed, her loss might well have turned her into an avenger, and her target all those non-widowed women, and he feared that her spleen might well embrace her daughter.

It was Cassie who rang the doorbell, and with a certain defiance. She had come solely to view the body, and until that time she could not settle into mourning. A stranger answered the door. She wore an apron and her hands were dusted with flour. She was clearly in charge of the funeral meats. She assumed a solemn face to match her calling, so that no mourner would mistake her spread for a party. She opened the door wide and directed them to the parlour. That door was closed, and it was Annie, with a sudden spurt of courage, who dared to open it. Her belly entered first, round and ripe, and it was this that met her mother's eye, that slapped her in the face almost, and that thundered the whole house into a terrible silence. Cassie and Will hovered in the doorway. On the table by the window lay the reason for their visit, the long brown box, its lid leaning on its side. Nobody moved and everybody looked at the floor. It was the widow herself who finally broke the silence and stillness. She rose, and Annie noticed how uncommonly tall she seemed, how that familiar victim's stoop had been shed, how even a smile appeared that might be construed as a welcome. But it was not a welcome for Annie. It was simply a smile that celebrated her own freedom. The freedom to wake up each morning without fear. Without fear that there was not a clean shirt for the master, ironed socks and vests. Without fear that the food she had prepared for him was tasty or otherwise, without fear of the sound of his key in the lock and the sudden spasm at the small of her back when she heard it. But that freedom did not embrace Annie.

'So you came,' she said, as her smile faded. She tried not to look at her daughter's offensive swelling. 'Now you're here, you might as well look at him. You can say goodbye.'

Annie hesitated.

'Go on,' her mother said, and practically pushed her towards the coffin. She wanted her daughter punished, though for what, she wasn't sure.

And then Annie felt ready to view him, not with sorrow or remorse, but simply to thank him from the bottom of her heart for dying and releasing them all.

They had tarted him up a bit. His cheeks were stuffed and slightly rouged, and his mouth, cotton wool stuffed where his dentures had been. He was dressed in his golfing gear, that in which he had no doubt died. Annie was glad that her mother had not insisted on a change to clean clothing. She had clearly written him off, and with no scruple. His clothes would go to a charity shop and had probably already been delivered. His personal effects would be sold for her mother would want no trace of him. The house, now mortgage-free, and his life insurance, together with his canny investments, would ensure a comfortable future, and for the rest of her life, her mother would be rooted to a battlefield that was familiar, but now without enemy. Occasionally she would miss him, and wonder where to put her hands.

Annie moved away from the box and motioned Aunt Cassie to the viewing. Cassie looked at her brother and said, 'So it's true.' She had never believed that, like everybody else, he was mortal. All his life he had advertised the myth that he was above all others. To this end he had bullied and blustered and black-mailed and his money had frightened open many locked doors. That he should die was inconceivable, and that he should be survived was not to be believed; survived by those who had suf-fered that self-generated myth that he was untouchable, and when Cassie said, 'So it's true', she was finally convinced that, despite the myth, he was mortal. 'I told you so,' she said under her breath and she turned away.

Then it was Will's turn. He tiptoed towards the coffin. Perhaps he thought that it was all too good to be true and that if he made a noise, his brother-in-law might wake up, grinning, having fooled them all. 'Rest in peace,' he said, because he felt he had to say something, but under his breath, 'Good riddance,' he whispered. He looked down at himself and he was ashamed of his funeral attire.

'Shall we all have a drink?' Annie's mother broke the silence. Her suggestion was a relief. It was a licence to them all to stop pretending. Let others mourn his passing, she seemed to be saying, those on the periphery of his life, who even had admired him, those who would miss the doors he'd opened for them and some of their wives perhaps who had been obliged to pleasure him for such favours. Let them mourn him and see him into the fire, and after a while realise with a certain pleasure that living was perfectly possible without him.

The funeral-meats lady was summoned with the drinks tray. Her face was a pall of disapproval. They might at least have waited until the coffin was sealed, she thought, before they par-tied. And if they could celebrate, she thought, so could she, a simple outsider and servant and, once back in the kitchen, she took a swig from the sherry bottle, and didn't even bother to re-cork it. By the time the undertakers arrived, the chief mourners were unsteadily jovial and as the men entered the parlour to seal the coffin, Will hid himself behind the sofa in case, in his attire, he might be mistaken for one of them.

And then Annie's mother did an extraordinary thing. She began to sing. She was, by nature, an unnatural soprano, and as such was never called upon to join a choir. For she could not hold a tune. Nevertheless, she chose that moment to notate her lungs. Perhaps she wanted to drown the noise of the hammers on the coffin, and had it been by way of a lullaby or a dirge, such a recital, even off-key, would have been admissible. But she chose a song that she must have recalled from her courting and dancing days, and the lyrics scurried round the parlour like a frenzied rat. 'I say tomato,' she sang, 'and you say tomayto. I say potarto and you say potato.' The undertakers looked up from their hammering and wondered at the nature of bereave-ment. Will, who sensed everyone's embarrassment, decided to join in with the song, hoping to dilute its eccentricity. But at least he could hold a tune and soon enough the tomatoes and the potatoes were back on an even keel. Shortly Cassie joined in, and then Annie, and the funeral-meats lady donated a descant from the kitchen and the undertakers matched their hammering with the rhythm of the song. When it was over, they all raised their glasses – the undertakers too, who in all their years of hammering had never seen the like – and it was a jolly party that almost danced through the front door into the waiting cars. The neighbours, net-curtain-glued, watched as Annie's belly jostled the box into the hearse. Poor soul, they thought, he's well rid of them, though the mourners would have argued that it was the other way round.

They sobered up a little during the drive to the cremato-
rium, but tears were far away and unlikely to arrive in time for
public viewing. There were few mourners in the chapel. For a
man who considered himself a pillar of the community, the
pews were appallingly empty. And for the first time since his
passing, his family began to feel sorry for him, and they prayed
that such bothersome pity would soon evaporate.

The vicar gave the standard address. He mentioned the
deceased's name, but apart from that particular, he could have
been talking about anybody. From somewhere an organ
donated appropriate music and the coffin, full of echoes of
tomatoes and potatoes, sailed ingloriously into the fire. Then
back home to the party along with other mourners whom Mrs
Dawson vaguely acknowledged.

The funeral-meats lady, half-seas over, opened the door for
them and ushered them into the parlour. The table that had
borne the box was covered now with appetisers. Will was given
the job as barman. Everybody was looking at Annie's belly, but
no one commented on its gross indecency. But they whispered
amongst themselves. 'It must have broken his heart,' they said.
'The shame of it. Disgusting.' And they stuffed their faces with
tuna and anchovy and slaked their thirst on the sweet sherry. As
soon as the decks were cleared, they saw no point in staying.
They mumbled their farewells and 'we're with you in your
sorrow', though there seemed little enough sorrow for them to
share, and they escaped with relief, anxious to mull over Annie's
belly on the pavement outside. The funeral-meats lady collected
her pay, and stuffed a full bottle of sherry into what she told
others was a tool-bag, but to herself, more of a loot-bag, and
she went home to put her feet up and pray for funerals.

Back in the house, for the first time since he had died, Annie's father was a positive absence, and indifference to his passing was slowly diluting. The fact that he heartily deserved to be forgotten was a sure guarantee that he would be remembered, and his family sat around silently, sober now and trying to get him off their minds. It was Annie's mother who suggested that they should all go to bed, although it was still early evening. 'We've had a trying day,' she said.

Nobody dissented, though none of them was tired. Each of them wanted to be alone to face or to fight the fiend of recall. Especially Annie. She had overheard the whisperings that she had broken her father's heart, and she wondered whether there was any truth in it. But true or not, it bothered her. Had she loved her father, and he her, she would have mourned his death and allowed time to heal her sorrow. But guilt prolongs grief and by that token she might never recover. Her baby kicked inside her and it felt like a punishment. She did not believe in reincarnation, but she heard herself praying that her child would be a girl. She went upstairs to her old bedroom, that room where she had loosened her buckled belt weekly and wondered what was to become of her. On her dressing-table was a picture of her father, proud in his golfing gear. It must have been taken in her prenatal absence, and her mother, with whatever motive, had placed it there. She picked it up and stared at it. 'I'm glad you're dead,' she said, 'and nothing's ever going to make me sorry.' Her baby kicked again, and Annie, fully-clothed, fell on to her bed, overcome suddenly by a blessed fatigue.

She was soon asleep, and when she awoke, expecting the morning light, it was still dark in her room. She wondered where she was, and why, and the reason for the simmering cauldron of pain in her belly. She called out and the light was on, with Cassie at her side and with Will on the phone for an ambulance, and with Annie's mother in the fearful doorway, praying that the child would be white.

It was a short labour. The baby was anxious to open her account, whatever that account would spell. And it was undeniably white and female. It didn't resemble anybody.

'She looks exactly like herself,' Will said and that put paid to any other speculation.

'I'll call her Mary,' Annie announced. She plucked the name out of nowhere and out of no one from whom the baby had come. Plain Mary she would be, unsired. And she would be loved with a passion that, in the end, would break Annie's heart.

Mrs Dawson took over the management of Mary from the start. She relinquished her at breast-feeding time, but otherwise she considered that the baby was in her sole care. Although Annie was not particularly happy with this arrangement, she saw its advantages. It gave her more time to study for the university exams.

'What are we going to tell her?' Mrs Dawson asked one evening after feeding-time.

'Tell her what?' Annie asked.

'About her father,' Mrs Dawson said. 'She'll want to know.'

'I haven't thought about it.'

'Well you'd better start thinking,' Mrs Dawson said. 'She's entitled to know.'

'I'll tell her the truth,' Annie said.

'Never.' Her mother put her foot down. 'She doesn't need to know that filthy truth.'

Annie thought she was speaking for her dead husband. Her

seemingly widowed freedom had not lasted long. 'What do you suggest then?' she asked.

'I've thought about it,' Mrs Dawson said. 'Her father was a soldier.'

'A private in the army during the war?' Annie suggested, though she was far from serious.

'Certainly not.' Mrs Dawson was not going to have a simple Tommy as a son-out-law. 'He was a Major and he was killed and buried in France. His name was Leonard Starkey.' She'd worked it all out. 'That's what we're going to tell her,' she said. 'We could make him a hero too. I could get hold of a medal. And a photograph.'

'You're preposterous,' Annie said, and thought no more of it. Until a week later, when she discovered a photograph of an officer on the nursery table and a medal hanging from its frame. She left it there, regarding it as a joke, too indifferent to argue. But she did nothing to scotch the story and as Mary grew, her grandmother told her the father tale, and by the time she was at school, she was a convinced daughter of a war-hero. It was too late for Annie to deny it, and perforce she had to collude. The man in the photograph was your father, she told Mary, and the medal was a token of his bravery. She told the story so often that she almost believed it herself.

One day at breakfast Mrs Withers was not to be seen. Annie stifled the unkind hope that she was not a con artist after all, but that an authentic terminal illness had carried her off during the night, and that there would be no more Cassandra mutterings at the table and everybody would be left to die in their own good time. But on enquiry Annie learnt that Mrs Withers had simply taken the day off and had been collected early that morning to be taken to her sister's house to celebrate her birthday, though of what number nobody was certain. Matron had guessed at eighty-five, and so had Mrs Withers' doctor. But the lady herself shyly admitted to no more than seventy, fearing that if the truth be known, people would think her old enough to die of natural causes. She had had a good innings, people would say of her, letting them off the hook of sympathy, which would have pleased Mrs Withers not at all. But at least her absence gave Annie a day's grace, and after Clemmie's daily visit that morning, she was able to socialise with others like herself who were travelling on the same journey.

It was Annie's third week at the hospice. If the doctor's prognosis was accurate, she could reckon on five weeks more. She had to admit that she did not feel well, that the passing of every day diminished her appetite and weakened her limbs. But with a mighty hand, it fed her talent for recall. But she was in no hurry. Almost seventy years of living could be recalled in one moment, but such speed had no respect for history. She savoured instalments and the relish or otherwise of each sequence. It was undoubtedly Freddie's turn, but for that instalment she needed to pause.

She took her seat in the dining room next to Mr Fenby. He had arrived at the hospice on the same day as herself, and equally as spry. But now he was in a wheelchair and although he sat at the lunch table, he only pretended to eat.

'How are you today?' Annie asked him.

He smiled at her. 'As you see,' he said. 'And you?'

'I think a lot,' Annie said. 'I recall.'

'There's no better time for remembering,' he said. 'The time we have left is a gift, a gift for that special purpose. D'you find it sometimes painful?' he asked.

Annie sensed that Mr Fenby was spending his remaining time in exactly the same way as she herself, and she felt close to him. She did not want to know the nature of his recall, nor did she expect him to reveal it, and she likewise, but it was enough to know that they were both measuring their allotted time in lovers, betrayers, past pains and joys. For such were the milestones of everybody's life and each hospice cubicle shuddered or sang with every recall.

'My son is visiting me today,' Mr Fenby said. 'But he won't share the past with me. "Plenty of time for that," he says. "We must think of the future," though he knows, poor boy, that for me there is no future. He refuses to acknowledge it. I feel so sorry for him. He's been difficult in his time. Given me lots of trouble. I try to convince him that I know that he loves me and loves me truly. My only regret is that I cannot live long enough to give him time to forgive me and thereby to forgive himself.'

Annie was startled. What Mr Fenby had said had stunned her, and like him, she wished for a longer time. A time for others to forgive themselves. Too late now for Freddie, and her bothering mother was also dead. But Mary. Mary. How many lifetimes would her Mary need to pardon herself, to know that she had loved and to acknowledge that she had been truly loved in return. She stroked Mr Fenby's hand. 'We are on the same journey,' she said.

The next morning Mr Fenby was missing from the breakfast table, but Mrs Withers was back in residence and in full harness, swearing that she had heard Mr Fenby's death-rattle in the middle of the night. Annie excused herself. On her way to her room, she met Mr Fenby's son in the corridor.

'I'm so sorry,' she said to him. 'Your father was a gentleman. He loved you very much, you know. And he knew that you loved him.' It was the least and the most that she could say.

When she reached her room, she sat on her bed and primped her hair. She had a blind date with Freddie.

It was Clemmie who arranged it all. Mary had just celebrated her second birthday. And in a man-less household. Annie's mother doted on her grandchild and laid down strict rules as to her upbringing. Annie wondered what her mother knew about upbringing, considering the sorry mess she had made with her own daughter. For Annie had never forgotten that rejection, that terrible silence that had made the choice between herself and her father. It rankled still, and would do, she feared, all her life. But she had to live with it and the daily abrasions that it entailed. Clemmie knew that her friend's marriage chances were slim. Few men would welcome a forerunner's intrusion, no matter how invisible he had become. But visible enough in the evidence that he had left behind. And she never tired of working behind the scenes to find a suitable match. She herself was involved with a saxophone player, but it was doubtful that the involvement was shared. Colin had his own combo, and occasionally he would invite Clemmie to a rehearsal. She would sit in the room directly in front of him and imagine her lips on the mouthpiece of his sax and that was what she meant by involvement. One day he told her that he'd discovered a singer and he wanted to try him out with the band.

'I think he's got something,' he said. 'We've got a gig on

Wednesday at the club, if you want to come. Bring Annie if you like. We could have a drink together afterwards.'

So Annie was brought. And Annie fell. At first sight, at first love, at first of everything. And so did Freddie. Their courtship began that very evening. They did not touch each other, but by their exchanged looks, they knew that they were bound. Towards the end of the evening, as they left the table in the club, Freddie's hand accidentally brushed Annie's bare arm, and love streaked her body like lightning. After that meeting they met daily and it took them a week to hold hands. They were so sure of each other that they knew they could take their time, convinced of a lifetime together.

Each night in bed, Annie would relive each touch and wonder whether she could ever be so happy again. She did not mention Freddie to her mother. She feared her reaction. In her grandmother and belated-mother roles, Mrs Dawson felt secure and content and she was unlikely to welcome any intrusion that would threaten the status quo. But Annie was anxious for Freddie to meet Mary. She had told him about Mary's provenance, as much of it as she could remember, but omitting a mention of the dark night of the GI truck, and he seemed unfazed by it. He himself was one of five children and, being the oldest of the family and the only boy, he had often played father and mother to his sisters. He told her about the little mining village in Wales where he was born. His father had been a miner until the pits had closed and then he had stayed at home cursing the silicosis until the day he died. He had made Freddie promise he would never go down a pit. 'You've got a voice, boy,' he would say. 'It will give you a living.' Freddie's teacher had told him so. In the school choir his boy's voice had soared like an angel, and even when it broke it held on to its wings. At seventeen, he'd won a singing scholarship to the Music Academy in Cardiff, where his teachers envisaged an operatic career. But then his father coughed himself out, and Freddie, ashamed of surviving him, went home to his mother to be the man in the house and to share its mourning. But singing all the time. He worked in a corner shop for a living but after a few years the village began to offend him. The sealed pit seemed to cock a snook in his face. Its closure had left the village community unanchored, the choirs had faded and the miners' clubhouse had closed. His childhood seemed to dwell in another time, another place and he had to leave, and quickly too, so that he could remember his village as it used to be in his father's time. So he went to London, disorientated but still singing. Loneliness threatened but was diluted by that stubborn song in his throat. And it was then that Colin heard him as they worked on the same conveyor-belt in the chocolate factory. The meticulous training was not lost on Colin's ear. Nor was the purity of the sound. Nor, above all, was the desperate need to be heard.

'I've got a combo,' Colin told him. 'You could sing with us if you like.' Colin knew his combo did not merit such a talent and when Freddie readily agreed and with such enthusiasm, he felt guilty. He tried him out in his own home, accompanying him on the piano, and he felt guiltier still. He desperately wanted him as part of his team but he knew that he could not keep such a voice for long, that others would hear him and, with sundry temptations, poach. It was a risk, but he would take it.

They had many rehearsals before Colin told Clemmie of his find.

'That's where you came in,' Freddie said.

'And will you stay with them?' Annie asked.

'As long as they want me,' he said. Freddie had no idea of his talent. He just wanted to sing. And any old song. *Don Giovanni* or the blues, as long as he could hear his voice which sang out his name, his village and, above all, his father.

Over the following weeks, as a direct result of Freddie's contribution, Colin was offered gigs all over the clubhouses of London. He feared their growing fame and the loss of its source. And perhaps it was to delay that loss or even to scotch it altogether that he found himself moving towards Clemmie in the hope of cementing a foursome that would never split. He was aware of a faint caddishness in his motives. He told himself that he was fond of Clemmie, but had he had the courage, he would have had to confess that he was far fonder of Freddie, and it was Freddie's lips that he wanted as his mouthpiece. He was aware that his was a cunning ploy and he disliked himself for it, but the thought of losing Freddie was more than he could bear. Thus it was that Clemmie's lips became his reluctant sax and her erstwhile term of 'involvement' had to seek another label. An 'item' was perhaps more suitable.

'Colin and I are an item,' she tried out on Annie one evening and Annie instinctively feared for her.

Three months had passed since their first meeting and Annie had still not taken Freddie home. But Mrs Dawson was suspicious. She was babysitting more often than hitherto. And Annie had changed. She seemed to have clutched at a new lease of life. She was studying hard for her exams. And although Mrs Dawson was pleased with this resolve, since it reinforced her position as minder and rearer, she feared the upshot of it all. She wondered whether Annie had found herself a man. And one evening, a rare evening when Annie was at home, she confronted her.

'His name's Freddie,' Annie said, 'and I love him. In time we're going to get married.' Now it was out. Now Freddie would have to be introduced, would have to meet Mary and weather her mother as well as he could. Mrs Dawson feigned pleasure, and asked to meet him.

He came on a Sunday, a day free of gigs or rehearsal. Mrs Dawson did not put herself out. The cake on the table was from the corner shop and looked stale. The sandwiches were still crusted, unlike her erstwhile meticulous entertaining. She did not even change her housedress and kept her apron firmly tied. Nor did she pay attention to Mary's attire. It was everyday and for no special occasion. Perhaps she hoped these signs of neglect would put off Annie's suitor. But when Freddie viewed the everyday appearance of the place, he felt immediately at home. He had feared that Annie's family would be posh and he would have felt ill at ease. He had brought Mary a present, a little doll, and she was shyly delighted with it, stretching out one hand to claim it, though clutching her grannie's skirt with the other. Grannie was satisfied. First blood to Mrs Dawson. There was no conversation at the table. If Mrs Dawson had taken Freddie seriously as a suitor for her daughter, she might have shown some curiosity as to where he came from. About his family perhaps, and his village and, above all, his prospects for the future. But she avoided enquiry, refusing to take the relationship seriously.

So Freddie himself volunteered. He told her about his village, his parents and his singing. And he sang a nursery song for Mary, who let go of her grannie's skirt. One all, Mrs Dawson inwardly scored, and she sensed that she was on a losing wicket. When tea was over, Freddie automatically rose to clear the table.

'There's no need for that,' Mrs Dawson said. Her tone was sour.

'I always did it at home,' Freddie said.

'But this is not your home,' she couldn't help saying. And unkindly. She was telling him that it would never be his home even if he cleared a thousand tables.

'It's just a habit,' Freddie apologised. 'I'm sorry.'

'Let's go to the park,' Annie said. She was enraged by her mother's behaviour and she would punish her by leaving her alone. 'Come along, Mary. Take Freddie's hand.' And they went out, the three of them, leaving Mrs Dawson seething at the uncleared table. The cake was almost untouched, as were the sandwiches, and she threw the lot in the bin to release her anger.

Once in the park, Annie was calmer. 'We'll get our own place,' she said. 'The three of us.'

'That would upset her,' Freddie said. 'She'd be lost without Mary.'

'She'd have to make a life for herself,' Annie said. 'In the long-run it would be for her own good. She might even marry again.' Though in her heart Annie knew that a remarriage was unlikely. Her mother had not enjoyed her first partnership and she would be wary of giving herself a second chance. Besides, Annie had to acknowledge the advantages of staying in the family home. As a full-time student, as she intended to be, she would need someone to look after Mary. And though she could afford to pay for someone out of the legacy her father had mistakenly left her – believing himself immortal he had never got round to changing his will – blood was thicker than water and, by the law of nature, should be more reliable. And there was no doubt that, having entirely negated her siring, Mrs Dawson loved Mary, and that love would more than take care of her.

'But will she ever accept you?' Annie asked.

'Of course she will, in time,' Freddie said. 'Who knows,' he laughed, 'she might even grow to love me.'

'I wouldn't want her to go that far,' Annie said, kissing his cheek. 'Only I am allowed to love you. And Mary.'

As it turned out, Freddie was right. In time, as he cleared table after table, after he fixed fuses, washers, leaks and 'no job too small', Mrs Dawson couldn't imagine how she'd ever managed without him and it was she who began to mention, in sideways fashion, the possibility of their marriage. But first Annie wanted to complete her university degree. Freddie was happy to postpone their marriage for a while, for he had been offered a spot with a well-established band that was to tour France and Germany. Colin wished him well, although he knew that his own combo had already lost its star. Freddie and Annie were so sure of each other that neither felt that any risk was entailed in a postponement. So Annie studied while Freddie toured. In time she completed her degree, as Freddie's career flourished. He was much in demand, and in the end he had to cancel a tour in order to find time enough to marry Annie and to take her on honeymoon.

From her hospice bed, Barbados was Annie's next stop. But not for long. It wasn't that they weren't happy together. Neither could ever imagine a more blissful time. It was simply curtailed because Freddie wanted to get back home. He said he was missing Mary. Annie was puzzled by his request. In later years, and without evidence, she would suspect its cause.

When the breakfast bell rang, it was with difficulty that Annie rose from her bed. And her poor appetite did not encourage her. But she was loath to withdraw from the dining room or the lounge, which adjoined it. She regarded them both as waiting rooms and as such, once left, could never be waited in again. Almost every morning Annie noticed a new face at the table and she tried to ignore those chairs that were empty. That morning, when she found it so irksome to leave her bed, Clemmie had arrived early. Perhaps she sensed her friend's fear of resignation, and she helped Annie to her feet and guided her down the corridor.

There were some faces she recognised, who were waiting there with waning appetites but with infinite patience. One face was shriekingly absent. Mrs Withers' chair was not only empty, it had been rudely removed. Annie called out her name. Mrs Withers was not allowed to be absent. She should never have been there in the first place. Everyone knew that. She was a con artist, a voyeur, with a gargantuan appetite for others' pain, and as such she was acceptable as a patient in disguise. But now, that morning, Mrs Withers proved to have been a genuine patient, and she had gone the way of all hospice flesh, called from the waiting room and rattled into the earth. 'Mrs Withers,' Annie called again. She felt let down. Betrayed. Mrs Withers had been an acceptable lie, but now she was revealed to be like all of them, bound for the terrible truth.

That morning Annie played with her breakfast and ate very little. Without Mrs Withers, the dining table had lost its *raison d'être* and Annie knew that she would not sit at it again. As Clemmie helped her out of the room, she made a point of not looking back. That would have been a gesture of farewell and a sign of her own abdication.

Clemmie settled her into her bed.

'How long have I been here?' Annie asked, as her friend tucked her in.

'About four weeks,' Clemmie said. It was more, at least six, which, according to the doctors, left only a fortnight's vigil. But Clemmie was reluctant to accept that prognosis.

'It's gone so quickly,' Annie said. 'I think that life speeds up as it reaches its end. I'm praying for time to remember. Everything. I don't want to cheat, Clemmie. I don't want to ignore certain events. I don't want to skip that which is too bothersome to recall. I want to recall it all. No matter how painful. And also to recall the joy. There was much joy, wasn't there, Clemmie?' She squeezed her friend's hand. 'Does Mary mention me?' Then she sighed with relief. An astonished relief. For she had actually put a name to the source of her despair. It was a beginning.

'I'm tired, Clemmie.' She wanted her friend to go. Not because she wanted to go to sleep, but because she had to go to Mary's prize-giving.

That was when Mary was in her last year at school. But there were many years before that time, Annie acknowledged, years of events that could be itemised and recalled without elaboration. Her own graduation, for example; Freddie's sell-out concerts and his unstoppable rise to fame; Clemmie's marriage and divorce. So many events to recall, such a jumble of memories, but now it was the prize-giving that claimed priority.

Mary with an award of a state scholarship to Oxford to read history. As Annie took Freddie's arm to help her into the car, there was a loud knock on her door.

'Just a moment, Freddie,' she whispered, as she asked her visitor to come inside. When she saw who her caller was, she stretched out her arms to embrace her. Mrs Withers, who had not forsaken her after all.

Mrs Withers was surprised at the affectionate reception; used all her life to being faintly disliked, she couldn't understand it at all. But it pleased her.

'I missed you at breakfast,' Annie said.

'I was in hospital. They took me in last night. Just for tests. Found nothing, of course. Just as I expected. So they sent me back here for a rest. You're back in bed, I see.'

Annie smiled. She no longer felt irritated by Mrs Withers' *schadenfreude*. She was glad that she was still around to enjoy her need. Mrs Withers, bless her, had resurrected herself. She was the truth, the life. She was also its consummate lie and her mendacity was the living source of hope.

'Welcome back,' Annie said. 'You smooth my path and I still "have miles to go and promises to keep". Come, Freddie,' she whispered, 'let us go.'

Annie loved going out with Freddie, because everybody looked at her. And she didn't mind. She was proud to be at his side, proud of their years together, of their enduring love that seemed unthreatened by his burgeoning fame. Freddie, for his part, was shy, disliking the limelight, and he walked with his head bowed, hurrying to a corner seat in the assembly hall where he was least exposed. Once there, he buried his face in the programme. He squeezed Annie's arm. 'It's a proud day,' he whispered, and Annie knew that Milwaukee, had he known, could not have been prouder.

The row in which they sat was shortly disturbed by Annie's

mother, who was not slow to bask in reflected glory. She had
driven her own car to the assembly, savouring her wealth and
independence, and though both were the result of the same
sour source – Mr Dawson's investments had multiplied over the
years – she flaunted them with relish.

'It's a proud day,' she whispered to Annie.

How lucky Mary was, Annie thought, to be the target of
such love and admiration. And it was a thought not without a
little envy for at seventeen, with her bursting buckled belt,
nobody had loved *her*, much less, despite her higher level dis-
tinction, offered her admiration. And the rejection that had
followed. Yes, it still rankled. She glanced at her mother sitting
by her side, and once again she heard that terrible silence that
spelt out her mother's choice between herself and her father.
She wondered if her mother ever recalled that day and sometimes she was tempted, in moments of spite, to remind her.

There was much business to be got through before the actual
award of the prizes. The headmistress opened the proceedings
with her report. Annie stared at her with rising bile. This was the
same woman who, in all her wisdom and purity, had refused to
recommend Annie for a university scholarship. 'Your daughter
has made her bed,' she told Mrs Dawson, 'therefore she must lie
on it.' And her parents had agreed and had certainly found her
a bed, but one that was far from home.

After the annual report, the school choir offered its minor
talent. Then the orchestra did likewise, and it became a wonder
that a school of such mediocre performance could produce a
state scholar. And when that was announced, the acclaim rang
with astonishment. Mary, who was seated in the front row of
the assembly, rose to collect her spoils, and as she mounted the
platform, she turned towards Annie and Freddie and smiled at

them. Then at her grandmother, who waved, confirming her presence to the audience. And afterwards they had slipped into a side-entrance and into a waiting car, which drove off as Freddie's fans were belatedly gathering.

'Who's my clever girl, then,' Freddie said, and he took Mary in his arms and hugged her. And Annie had watched and thought that Freddie was a good man and a kind man. And an innocent.

That summer, Freddie was touring in Europe and the three Dawson women took a cottage in Cornwall. It was a peaceful time. Mrs Dawson had mellowed over the years. She seemed to have totally forgotten that day of her silence. Or perhaps she denied to herself that it had ever happened, because she simply couldn't understand why Annie occasionally lost her temper with her for no apparent reason and would hurl insults without apology. She couldn't understand it at all. 'She takes after her father,' she would whisper to herself. 'She's a bully. Just like him.' Yes, she'd forgotten that silence, that silence of rejection. She had never heard it. How was one supposed to hear a silence, anyway? Yet somewhere deep inside she knew that it was there. That it was that silence that prompted Annie's insults and abrasiveness. But most days were free of Annie's tetchiness. For the last weekend Freddie joined them, before they returned to London to prepare Mary for leaving home.

Home was no longer that house of the silence. Freddie's income had afforded a larger house with an annexe that was a luxurious grannie flat, where Mrs Dawson was supposed to spend most of her time. But on days when Annie was calm and friendly, she chose to spend it in the main house. And she was there for Mary's send-off. She sat on Mary's bed and watched her packing. Mary modelled all her new clothes for her grannie's approval, which she gave with words but not with her heart.

She'd heard the phrase 'generation gap' and she found it useful
to explain why she found Mary's wardrobe so unappealing. And
Annie's too, though the gap was narrower, yet still a chasm
that had more to do with history than with age.

Mary had begged Freddie to drive her to Oxford, though she
knew that he avoided any public appearance that was not
entailed in his career. But Mary, like her mother, loved to bask
in Freddie's fame, in his voice, his looks and his sheer presence.
So Freddie had yielded and because Annie sensed that Mary
wanted Freddie to herself on that day, she and her mother
waved them off in the car.

Suddenly the house seemed strangely empty. And depress-
ingly silent. And for some reason Annie felt unsafe. She stared at
her mother with one of those looks that Mrs Dawson had learnt
was a prelude to a temper, and she withdrew quickly to her
annexe. Annie wondered at her uncertainty. There were no reasons for it. Freddie was as loving as always. His career was more
than prosperous. Her own too, since she had landed a fine
teaching job. Perhaps it was because of all those blessings that
she was suddenly aware of the possibility of loss, and that aware-
ness prompted a premature mourning. She made herself some
coffee and, as she drank it, she timed Mary's journey to Oxford
and she watched Freddie as he carefully manoeuvred the country lanes, for he would have avoided the direct, speedy route.
She guessed at their conversation, then aware of invasion into
privacy, she blocked her ears until they reached Oxford. Then
Freddie alone on his return journey and she timed him, eagerly
awaiting his arrival. Which was sooner than she had expected
because he had driven direct, anxious for home and Annie.

Together they weathered Mary's absence. She would be
home for Christmas, and Freddie would not work on that day.

So Annie happily made preparations. The decorations, the food and the presents. And then, as they all sat down for Christmas dinner, they reached for their crackers and Mary handed hers to her grannie, as pulling partner. It was then that Mary, even with a happy smile, dropped her bombshell, and the noise of the crackers, loud as they were, did little to drown her words or their horrendous matter.

Annie listened, deafened. Then fled from the memory. Back to the hospice, her refuge and her strength, where the past was not imperative, and the friendly present promised no future.

A nnie waited impatiently for Clemmie to come. Now, bed-bound, she missed the gossip, the dining room's goings-on. News of the waiting list for those who were queuing to die, news in which she was basically totally uninterested, but which would anchor her to her present circumstances and hopefully preoccupy her to the point of blocking out the past. Clemmie would tell her everything. She was in Matron's confidence.

When she arrived, Annie was struck by the smile on her friend's face. For it was unnatural, forced, and was clearly manu-factured to veil the real reaction that Annie's appearance evoked. Since her arrival at the hospice, Annie had avoided mirrors, knowing that her fading condition would be reflected in her face. She had always been vain, and had had the looks that pleased. Occasionally, while in bed, she would run her fingers over the contours of her face and find little that disturbed her. It was still wrinkle-free, which pleased her, but her fingers could not decipher her colour, which was yellowing and sour. But her welcoming smile to Clemmie was true, for more and more she loved her friend as she realised that Clemmie was possibly the only person in the world who would miss her when she was gone. But that thought bred others, that of Mary, and of Freddie, whom she had forgotten was already dead. She did not want such thoughts. She wanted the present, the safe present where nothing could touch her further.

'What news?' she asked. She was almost shouting, drowning those thoughts that she could not entertain. 'Is Mrs Withers still in the dining room?'

It was clearly the most urgent question to ask, and its answer most eagerly and fearfully awaited.

'I saw her just now,' Clemmie lied. 'She was leaving the dining room.' Clemmie knew that on no account was Mrs Withers to be known to die. That as long as Annie was alive, Mrs Withers would always be there, conning Matron and the whole office staff with her disguise.

'It's strange she hasn't been to visit me.'

'I heard Matron has discouraged her,' Clemmie improvised. 'She thinks that drop-in visitors can be a disturbance.'

'A disturbance to what?' Annie smiled. 'I'm not that desperately busy.'

'How are you feeling?' Clemmie was desperate to change the subject, but enquiry into her friend's health was no change at all.

'I'm dying,' Annie said. 'That's how I'm feeling. Let's change the subject.'

'Bonnie is getting a divorce,' Clemmie said. Bonnie was Clemmie's god-daughter, married for twenty years and every one of them threatening divorce. 'This time she's serious,' Clemmie said. 'He's left her and she's selling the house. I'm glad about it really.'

'I don't understand it,' Annie said. 'Why do people stay together for so long if they're so unhappy. But they do, Clemmie. You of all people know they do. But, like you, they hope. They live in hope that things will change.'

Clemmie shivered with recollection. Now it was *her* wish to change the subject. They were both perilously close to delving into the past and they wanted none of it. But between two friends who had known each other for so long there was no conversation piece that did not, in some way, invoke the past. And for a moment Annie wished that Clemmie would leave and cease to threaten her with recall. But then she would be on her own and there would be no voice at all to silence the past and she would be stranded with it, alone and screaming. For a moment, she wished that she could die, and quickly, for only death could still those memories that were so painful.

'Scrabble?' Clemmie asked. She was already arranging the board on the bedside table. But Annie didn't want to play. She preferred the jigsaw. Clemmie had brought it when Annie had first moved into the hospice. It was a complicated piece, with much sky and with undefined nebulous cloud. From the dark corner of the picture, it seemed that a storm was brewing and she was not surprised when she heard the rain lashing the window panes. Again she wished that Clemmie would go away, because jigsaw-solving was a solitary pursuit.

And Clemmie read her thoughts. 'It's raining,' she said. 'They say there'll be a storm. I'd better get back. We can Scrabble tomorrow.' She kissed her friend, just a delicate peck on the forehead, for anything more lasting might have signalled a real farewell. But there would be a tomorrow and a tomorrow after that. Pecking time, until the tomorrows ceased.

When she had gone, Annie pondered the jigsaw. She had

completed about a quarter of it and she was taking her time. She sensed that death would not call her while there was still unfinished business to attend to. She planted a piece in the corner where the cloud was gathering, and as she did so, a loud clap of thunder shook the window panes; although she tried her level best not to equate the sound with Mary's bombshell, she was shipped right back to that Christmas table, and Mary's innocent thunderbolt.

'I want to visit my father's grave,' she said. 'You have to help me find it. All I know is his name.'

Mrs Dawson's cracker was only half pulled and she handed it to Mary. First things first, she thought, and last too, for there was no help that any of them could offer.

'Why now?' Freddie asked. 'You've never mentioned it before.'

'There was a programme on the wireless about special days for relatives to visit the war cemeteries. I've got three weeks' vacation. I thought I'd go to France. Will you help? Or maybe you'd like to come with me.'

Annie looked at her mother with hatred. It had been her bloody idea in the first place. But she said nothing. Neither did Freddie. He knew that Mary had been deceived, but he felt that it was none of his business.

'Well?' Mary asked. She didn't understand their silence. She looked at her mother for some response. But how could Annie tell her the truth? For years she had managed never to recall that evening in the truck when Mary was conceived. But now she could not erase it.

It was a Saturday night. Her exams were over and she had done well. She was going out with Molly and Ruth, her classmates. Annie had no difficulty in remembering their names and for some reason that offended her, for their identities should have been left in the back of that truck, along with Milwaukee. They met at the church hall. Final hospitality night for the GIs before they embarked for home. 'Don't be late,' their mothers had told them, as if an early night was all that was called for to ensure their good behaviour. The girls had been to such hospitality nights before, always with their mothers, to help them with cakes and sandwiches. But that night, since it was the last of its kind, had been catered. There was a three-piece band and there were many couples on the dance floor. There were more girls than boys in the hall and they wall-flowered the room pretending not to care. But Annie and her friends were lucky.

'What's your name?' Annie asked.

'Call me Milwaukee. That's where I come from.'

Slow, slow, quick quick slow around the room, closer and closer on the turns, and guided, panting, out of the hall and into the yard where the trucks were parked. And, behind them, Ruth and Molly, still quick-stepping. And quickly they're climbing into darkness. Annie thought that it would be just the top half of her that would oblige him, like it did in the back row of the pictures when she went on a Friday night with Ricky. But Milwaukee was going home the next day and he wouldn't have to stay around to apologise. It was not the top of her body that he was after. In fact he didn't touch it. She heard movements from the far end of the truck where presumably Molly and Ruth were being seen to, and because she had no choice she let Milwaukee see to her as well. Then the weight lifted and there was a scuffle and the three GIs bolted

into the darkness, leaving their receptacles behind. There was
quiet then. Not a word was spoken. Shame had stifled their
voices. Thereafter they avoided each other, these once close
friends, but of them all, only Annie had a belt-buckle problem.
She looked at Mary across the table. How could she, so pub-
licly and in such cold blood, tell her daughter that she had no
idea of her father's name, nor even a remembrance of his face.
Or tell her of the dark innards of the truck, that ignoble site of
her origins. But an answer was claimed, demanded almost, by
the silence around the table.

'We lied to you,' Annie said at last. 'Grannie and I. We made
up your father. We thought we ought.'

'You made up the Major?' Mary was stunned. 'The hero?
The medal? The photograph? I boasted about him in school. I
got on people's nerves with my bragging. My hero Daddy.'
She was spitting with rage. 'Then who is my father, for God's
sake? My real father.'

'I don't know,' Annie said helplessly. 'I never knew. He was
American. He said he came from Milwaukee. I'm sorry,' she
said, though she knew from Mary's look of horror that a lifetime of sorrys would not be enough.

'You're disgusting,' Mary managed after a while.

Suddenly she looked like her grandfather when a flush of
Christian values would occasionally disturb him. And when she
made to rise, Annie half expected her to go and stand in front of
the fire.

'It wasn't my fault,' Annie whispered.

'Why didn't you tell me?' Mary shouted.

'Because I was ashamed.'

It was then that Mary realised that she only half-knew herself.
That there were certain traits in her nature that she had always

wondered at. She was quarrelsome, for example, and she kept few friends, and then there were her sudden rages and bitterness, none of which characteristics she could have inherited from her mother. She suspected that her real father was not one she could admire or even learn to love, but it was imperative that she trace him, if only to understand that half-shadow of herself. And her slut of a mother didn't even know his name.

'Milwaukee,' she said with contempt.

'It's in the State of Wisconsin,' Mrs Dawson offered, as if that might help.

'Aren't you a clever old thing then,' Mary said. 'I'm going to find him, wherever he is.'

'You never will,' Freddie said. His voice was raised. 'He might not even be from Milwaukee. He was probably lying. So forget about him. He couldn't have been worth very much.'

'He's half of *me*,' Mary said. 'And the other half is a slut. So how much am *I* worth?'

'We love you,' Annie said. 'All of us. Is that not enough?'

Mary rose from the table. 'I'm not hungry,' she said, and she left the room.

Annie knew that her link to Mary was now for ever frayed, and possibly would soon be severed. She found it hard to hold back her tears. But Mrs Dawson was unmoved, and Annie viewed her mother's unaffected appetite as a betrayal.

Somehow the meal was consumed. The sprouts, the bread-sauce, the chestnut stuffing. The pudding was brandied and lit, and the hidden sixpenny pieces discovered without pleasure. The meal was a mere duty to be done. Christmas had been dealt with. They need not listen to the carols on the wireless, nor to the Queen's speech. They need not sit together as a family to open their presents. That would have been too embarrassing and would have called for apologies that were not meant at all.

Freddie started to clear the table. He knew that, with Mary's outburst, things could never be the same again. A sense of family had been shaken and he didn't know how to handle it. He felt an outsider, yet he felt, too, that he was somehow the cause of Mary's rage. Since she was a baby, he had treated her like his own daughter. She had trusted him. Now she would view him as part of that deception. He had colluded in all those 'hero' lies. She must surely hate him.

'I'm going to my room,' Mrs Dawson said. 'I want to hear the Queen.' She looked at Annie, whose tears did not affect her. She opened her mouth to speak, to utter a phrase that no doubt had pickled on her tongue ever since the day Annie's belt-buckle had burst. She had heard it from her husband, and now she echoed it. 'One's chickens come home to roost,' she said, smiling a little, pleased that the saying was out at last, though half of those chickens were hers in the first place. With that parting shot, she left the room, and quickly, it seemed, for her own safety.

Freddie took Annie in his arms. 'It will mend,' he said, though he knew that the rift was beyond repair.

For the rest of that Christmas holiday, Mary was rarely seen; sometimes she disappeared for days on end. Annie didn't know where she was sleeping. Then suddenly she'd return and sulk and fly into tempers, and Annie wished her away again, but Mary stayed put, as if to spite her.

Freddie was booked into a new band for a Netherlands tour. He asked Annie to come with him but she declined. Despite Mary's sulks, she was fearful for her and didn't want to leave her alone. So she weathered the week without Freddie, but she felt unsafe, unanchored, and although there was no question of her love for Mary, she had to own that she didn't like her very much. She longed for Freddie to come home, but she was wary too of his return.

In her hospice bed, Annie dreamt of Milwaukee. Just the name, not the place of it. She dreamt of its separate letters, especially the double 'ee' at its end. When she woke she realised that the word and its letters had played no part in her thinking for many years; as if from the very beginning it was so faintly written that only a short time was needed to erase it entire. But now, post-dream and wide awake, Annie saw the letters still, this time in her father's office, the room at the top of the house, which served his business concerns. Some weeks after Mary was born, her mother had taken the baby to the park and for the first time since her return from Sheffield, Annie was alone in the house. She felt free, with a sense that nobody was looking, that she could do what she wished and no one would ever find out. In other words she could satisfy that urge to rummage in her father's office. She did not know what she was looking for. Perhaps she hoped for a clue to some act of kindness that would redeem him a little. She crept up the stairs into the attic and straight to his desk. The file was marked 'Personal', and the letter was on top of the pile, but not yet clipped into place. It was dated only a few days before her father's death, so he had not got round to dealing with it. And when Annie read it, she was once more delighted that he had died.

It was addressed from the rectory of their local church and

signed by the vicar, that vicar who had feigned to know so little about her father at his funeral when clearly he had known a great deal more.

'Dear Mr Dawson,' Annie read.

I'm sorry that it has taken some time to get back to you, but at last I am able to furnish you with more details regarding your request. I managed to trace the visitors' book which covered the date you mentioned. As you know we insisted on guests' signatures on entry to our hospitality events. That last was particularly crowded as I remember and the names are hurriedly written, and not all of them are legible. There seems to be only one from Milwaukee, which is a blessing, I suppose. His name is Jimmy, probably James Winer and his serial number is 770968. That's all the information he gave, but I imagine it is enough for you to trace him. It's possible of course that there were others who didn't sign the book and those might have included one or more from Milwaukee, but alas I have no trace of them. As to Winer's colour, I cannot advise you. We were obliged to admit coloured servicemen although it was strictly against my policy. I thought that they should have made their own arrangements, but I was overruled. I share your shame. You have not deserved it. You can count absolutely on my silence. I am mindful of the great favour you afforded me not long ago for which I shall be for ever grateful. And as you have kept my confidence on that score, I shall do likewise with yours.

Yours faithfully,
Victor Wainwright.

When Annie had finished reading, she found herself less surprised at discovering Milwaukee's identity than she was curious
about the favour her father had granted the vicar. He had paid
off a blackmailer perhaps, to redeem the negatives of some tell-
tale photographs? Or arranged an abortion for one of the vicar's
mistakes? Annie favoured the first possibility. Picturing the vicar,
she thought he was unlikely to have a woman on the side. He
was a bit like Colin perhaps, with forbidden appetites.

It was almost twenty years since she had read that letter and
she had put his possible name out of her mind. Absolutely. In
the back of the truck, he would have answered to the name of
Milwaukee, and had any words broken that humping silence,
Milwaukee he was, and ever more would be so. And when Mary
had asked for her father's name at the Christmas table, she had
spoken the truth. She had erased the vicar's letter from her
mind. Milwaukee was all she could offer, and Milwaukee would
have to do. She put the letter back in the file, and wiped her
hands of its filth.

Then her memory vaulted the years, for recall has no respect
for chronology. She remembered waking up one morning.
Freddie was on tour and Mary was leaving that day to go back
to Oxford. She rose quickly to make her some breakfast. It
would be a silent one, she knew, for the two did not speak.
Mary acted like a sullen lodger, and Annie as her reluctant land-
lady. In the kitchen she saw that breakfast of a kind had already
been eaten. The table was strewn with dirty plates and the cloth
was marmalade-stained. In the midst of the mess lay a note. A
no-beating-about-the-bush note, a fuck-you note.

Gone to Milwaukee,
    Mary.

She wanted Clemmie to come. Then she remembered that she was in Brighton that day to be with Bonnie at her divorce hearing. She would have to face a whole Clemmie-less day with nothing to do but to read that note over and over again.

She waited for her mother to arrive. Perhaps she could offer some explanation. But when lunchtime came and Mrs Dawson, whose daily habit it was to take breakfast in the main house, still had made no appearance, Annie sniffed the sour smell of collusion. So she went to the annexe, prepared to do battle.

'Mary's gone,' she shouted at the door and made for the sitting room, where her mother sat playing patience. With one thrash of her arm, Annie swept the cards off the table. 'You knew,' she shouted. Her mother bent down to collect the cards but she said nothing. Annie kicked them out of her reach. 'Answer me,' she shouted.

'Yes, I knew,' Mrs Dawson said. She spoke with the calm of a conqueror. 'I told her where to find him.'

'Milwaukee's a big place,' Annie said bitterly, 'and he might have been lying.'

'He wasn't lying,' Mrs Dawson said. Once again she attempted to gather the cards, and once again Annie kicked them aside.

'How do you know?'

Mrs Dawson heard the fear in her daughter's voice and it did not displease her. 'After your father died,' she said, 'I found a letter from Reverend Wainwright. There was a register of guests at that hospitality night. Only one from Milwaukee. Jimmy Winer.'

Even as her mother was speaking, Annie recalled every word of that letter, every word that over twenty years had blurred. And her mother had kept that name on the tip of her vicious tongue until it ripened and fell. Fell to destroy a family, one that, in its unshared ignorance, had managed to achieve occasional bliss.

'I gave the name to Mary. I thought she was entitled,' Mrs Dawson concluded. Once again she bent down to gather the cards and this time Annie didn't prevent her.

'Weren't you satisfied the way things were?' Annie almost whispered. 'Was it not good enough for you that you had a fine home and people to care for you? Did you stop for one moment to think of the consequences? I hope to God she doesn't find him. I hope to God he's dead. And if he isn't I hope to God you'll live to be sorry.'

Mrs Dawson was once more laying out the cards on the table, calmly, as if her game had never been interrupted. 'Mary was entitled,' she said again, and having grown fond of the word, would call on it in her defence whenever it was required. 'Entitled,' she said again and again to herself, until she felt she had invented it.

Annie went back to her kitchen and sat at the table that was covered with the dishes Mary had left for her to clear. She read the note again, hoping perhaps to find a hidden message. But it was a one-liner, so that there was no possible reading between the lines. It meant exactly what it said, and no good could possibly come of it. But the alliance that her mother had struck with Mary gave her a vestige of hope. Mary would write to her grandmother and give a progress report of her search. Or, more likely, its dead end. There would be some contact and her mother would not be so cruel as to withhold any news she had received.

Mrs Dawson resumed her breakfasts in the main house and there were no signs that she had anything up her sleeve and Annie was too proud to ask if there had been any news from

Milwaukee. Until one morning, about a month after Mary had left, she was late for breakfast, and she wore an unnerving smile. Annie read it as an I-told-you-so smile and she was glad that Freddie was at the table to share whatever news that smile implied. She had told him about the vicar's letter, and it had disturbed him.

Mrs Dawson took her time. She buttered her toast and spread the marmalade, all the while smiling with a smile that begged to be asked what it was for. But Annie wouldn't oblige. It was Freddie who asked her what she was so pleased about. And Annie was relieved.

'I had a letter from Mary this morning,' Mrs Dawson said, and she gave her smile a rest and assumed a solemn look that meant she had news of import.

'From Milwaukee?' Freddie asked, sensing that, in her pride, Annie would give her mother no word of encouragement.

'Yes. From Milwaukee,' Mrs Dawson said.

'What does she say?' Freddie was impatient.

Mrs Dawson stared at Annie. 'Are *you* not interested in what Mary says?'

'If you want to tell me,' was all Annie would give her.

'Well, I think if she were *my* daughter, I'd be very interested to hear that she'd found her *real* father.'

'*Found* him?' Freddie could not believe it.

Annie could no longer hold her tongue. 'Where?' she shouted.

'Ah, a little interest at last,' Mrs Dawson said, deeply enjoying herself, and both Freddie and Annie thought what a mean and unpleasant person she was.

'In Milwaukee,' Mrs Dawson said. 'Exactly what he told you.'

'Where's the letter?' Freddie asked.

'It's in my room.'

'Can we see it, then?' Freddie asked again.

But Annie knew that her mother was playing a power game and she was not going to encourage it. 'We don't need to see it. Just tell us what it says.'

'Like I told you, she's found her real father. Jimmy Winer. He's divorced with no children. And she likes him.' She paused before dropping her bombshell. 'He wants to see you, Annie, and he's coming back with Mary.'

'He'll be lucky,' Annie managed a laugh. 'I never want to see him again. You arranged all this,' she turned on her mother, 'you see it through.'

'Annie's right,' Freddie said, and they left the room together.

'You'll have to meet him,' Freddie said when they were alone. 'For Mary's sake. You just have to acknowledge him as her father.'

'But I don't even remember what he looked like. He may not even be her real father. There were others there that night who didn't sign in, but who could have been from Milwaukee.'

'But Mary seems convinced.'

Annie gave in. 'I'll see him,' she said.

Her mother was going to see friends for tea that afternoon and while she was away Annie went to the annexe in search of Mary's letter. She had no scruples about her intrusion. She was, to use her mother's favourite word, entitled to see her daughter's letter. She found it easily enough, lying in its envelope on the patience table. The postmark confirmed that it was from Milwaukee. She extracted the letter carefully and held back a tear as she recognised Mary's handwriting. 'Dear Grannie,' she read, 'I've found him.' A number of exclamation marks followed.

He really is James Winer. He used to be married, but not any more. He says he's never forgotten my mother.

Where was 'Mum'? Annie wondered.

I told him about Freddie and he got so excited because he has all his records. He says he wants to see her again – you know who I mean – but he's pretty poor I think, and can't afford the airfare. So I offered to pay for him, and I'm bringing him back with me. He's dying to meet you, Grannie, and he's grateful that it was you who helped me to find him. I'll be back soon. I'll have to wait for Dad!!! to get his passport. Then we'll come home. I'll let you know when.
    Love Mary.

Annie sweated with the dread of meeting him. I will acknowledge him, she decided, and then I will tell him to go away. I cannot be expected to house him. Having made that decision, she might have relaxed a little. But she had no idea how long it would be before she had to confront him or whether, indeed, her mother, out of her natural spite, would keep their arrival secret and catch Annie unprepared.

But Annie guessed the dreaded time had come on the morning Mrs Dawson failed to appear for breakfast. She was not in the annexe and Annie supposed that, at such an early hour, she had gone to the airport to meet them. She returned to the house and shared her fears with Freddie.

'I heard a cab outside about seven o'clock,' he said. 'I didn't want to wake you.'

'She's gone to meet them,' Annie said.

Freddie put his arm around her. 'We'll face it together,' he said.

'No.' Annie was resolved. 'I'll see him alone. And without Mary.' She would grill him. She would give him a bad time. She seethed with hatred of him, and marvelled that out of such loathing Mary could have flowered.

They sat for a while at the table while silence lay between them. They heard the morning paper fall through the letter-box, but neither moved to collect it. Both were waiting for the sound of the cab, and when it came Annie fled the kitchen with no place to hide. Then she heard a cry, a cry that came out of her sleep of her Milwaukee dream, a cry that forbade further recall. 'No more, no more,' it mouthed, and when she opened her eyes, it was a blessed relief to see the curtains of her cubicle and to feel the doctor's hand on her arm.

He had the sense not to ask her how she was feeling. Instead he said, 'How are you coping?'

'I'm trying to get my mind off my mind,' she said.

He smiled. 'Difficult with a mind like yours. He shifted in his chair. He seemed ill at ease. He had run out of words and there was nothing he could practically do. There was no point in examining her. He did not unfold the sheet that covered her. He knew that her legs were swollen, and yellow like her whole body. Even to take her pulse or blood pressure would have seemed a sham and Annie would have known it.

'You are very brave to come,' she said. 'You play Scrabble?' she asked. She wanted to put him at his ease.

He was grateful for the suggestion. 'We can have a quick

game,' he said, 'though like most doctors, my spelling is atrocious.'

He laid out the board and they helped themselves to the letters. They played slowly. The doctor, whose spelling was as unreliable as he had owned, was inclined to phonetic display and his show of hopeful words made Annie laugh. Sometimes she corrected him, but at other times she let his blunders lie. As a result the score was more or less equal. Until Annie's last throw. It was a simple four-letter word. Taxi, and its 'X' had landed on a triple.

'I reckon I'm well and truly beaten,' the doctor said. He looked up from the board and saw a sudden pallor on Annie's face and she had begun to tremble. Automatically he took her pulse and it was racing. He found himself wishing that its speed would overwhelm her, that however she must protest, it would race her into oblivion. For a lingering death is a hindrance. It recalls less joy than regret, less comfort than remorse, less peace than self-reproach and he knew that that was why Annie was trying to get her mind off her mind.

'I'm tired,' she whispered. But she was not tired at all. She had one of the hardest miles to go and she could only travel alone. She had heard the taxi with its triple score, and she had to pay attention. It was no use trying to hide and Freddie was gently guiding her back to the kitchen, as the doctor was leaving the room.

Freddie sat her back down at the breakfast table. He held her hand as they waited in silence for the sound of the bell. But instead they heard a key in the lock. Mrs Dawson's key, asserting its proprietary rights. She entered the kitchen alone.

'Are you ready?' she said. It was her show. She was its pro-
ducer and impresario. Freddie stood up. But not Annie. She
didn't trust her feet.

'Mary?' the show-woman called. Mary first, because she
was no stranger to anybody. Mrs Dawson was keeping her
discovery till last. She left a pause for some reaction to Mary's
return.

'Welcome home,' Freddie said and went towards her. But
Mary did not move, or smile or even look at him. It seemed that
she would not acknowledge that he was even there. Annie
didn't move. She was pleased that Mary had returned but she
was in no mood to welcome her home. Mary ignored her lack
of welcome, and she turned towards the door.

'Dad?' she called.

Freddie returned to his seat. He tightened his jaw in a flush
of anger. He felt displaced. Mary's call had, with little ceremony, given him the sack. He looked at Annie and she
motioned him to sit down at his customary seat at the head of
the table. Thus she confirmed his status, and took his hand.

'Dad' was dawdling, and there was a short interval before he
made his debut. Then, nervously, he stood in the doorway for
their inspection. He tried a smile, but sensing that it would not
be welcome, he gradually assumed a serious expression.

'It's great to meet you all,' he said, for he thought he ought
to say something, though nothing he could think of was appropriate. He weathered the silence that followed, together with
the look of disgust on Annie's face. He presumed that that
stern woman, so firmly seated at the table, was the one they
called Annie, for he had never seen her in his life before. And
neither had Annie seen him. She could barely remember
Milwaukee's face, having seen it only in the dim light of the

dance floor and the semi-darkness in the back of the truck, but
she knew with total certainty, and with a spasm of womb
instinct, that this Milwaukee was not Mary's father. She stared
at him in silence. He was a handsome man without doubt. She
wondered where and how Mary had found him, and wondered
too whether Mary was so desperate for a father that any
Milwaukee would do.

Mrs Dawson broke the silence. 'I'll make a pot of coffee,' she
said. She was taking over and enjoying every moment of it.

'I'll make it,' Annie said, rising quickly from her seat. She
wanted to get out of the room, away from its fraud and deception, but she could not help but admire his shameless nerve. She
wondered how he would face it out, and what he had to gain
from his deceit. Above all, she wondered about her mother and
what she hoped to gain from her part in it. Since Mary's
Christmas bombshell, Mrs Dawson had undergone a change.
She was slowly reverting to the wife she had once been, the
bitter one, the silent and mean one, bent on what seemed like
revenge. But for what? Annie wondered, and could only con-
clude that it was envy of her own happiness with Freddie. She
heard the talk through the open door.

'I'm sure honoured to meet you,' Milwaukee was saying.
'I've been one of your fans for years.'

'He's got all your records,' she heard Mary say. She didn't
hear Freddie's response and presumed it was silence.

'Sit down,' her mother was saying. 'We can move the luggage
later. Annie wondered where Milwaukee was supposed to sleep.
She certainly would not invite him into the house. He could
stay in the annexe. Her mother had probably already invited
him and she wondered again what plan her mother had in mind.
She would not wish to displace Freddie who, after all, was

something of a golden goose. Perhaps she genuinely believed that this Milwaukee was the real one and even if he wasn't, he was enough to make Mary happy. She decided that she would get the imposter on his own, that she would feign a poor memory and ask him to recall their so-called courtship. Would the dance floor figure? Or the back of the truck? She smiled to herself. She rather looked forward to the grilling.

She took the coffee pot into the breakfast room. She decided that she would be friendly and hospitable. She would give him the impression that he had gotten away with it, and then the more spectacular would be his undoing.

'Did you have a good flight?' she asked, when the coffee had been poured.

Mary was fooled by her mother's sudden warmth, and she became voluble, describing the scenes at Chicago airport, the flight, the food and the bumpy landing. Annie concluded that Mary was quite a bore. So was her obvious happiness and she wondered whether she had the right to disillusion her. After the flight recital, Mrs Dawson detailed her ride to the airport and her waiting time in Arrivals. She too was a dreadful bore, Annie thought, but she weathered it all with a fixed smile. Then Freddie rose from the table. He had a rehearsal, he said, though Annie knew his day was free. She felt his discomfort and, as he was leaving, she followed him to the door and kissed his cheek for reassurance.

When he had gone, Mary uttered a loud sigh. 'Now we can talk,' she said.

Annie was outraged. She resented the idea that Freddie's absence would give Mary a sense of relief and freedom.

'You'd better take your bags to the annexe,' she said. 'Go with Grannie. I'd like a word with our visitor.'

'My dad,' Mary said. She kissed him on his cheek. 'I'll see you soon.'

When they had gone, Milwaukee rose to gather the plates. And Annie was reminded of Freddie's attempt all those years ago to clear the table, and how her mother had strictly forbade it. 'There's no need for that,' Annie said. 'Sit down. I'd like to talk to you. About old times.' She smiled at him. She wanted him at his ease. He took his seat again and he looked nervous. He had expected a grilling of sorts. He had gleaned little enough information from Mary herself and he was not looking forward to their one-sided recall.

'My memory's awful,' Annie laughed, 'and it was all such a long time ago. Do you remember any of it?' she asked kindly.

'Why didn't you let me know about Mary?' he said. He sounded angry. 'It's the least you might have done.'

'I didn't have your address,' she said. She omitted the fact that she didn't even know his name.

'You could have gotten it from Army registers. Easy. I heard lots of English broads did that. Same thing. And they didn't have to be pregnant. You should have told me.'

She marvelled at his nerve and she wondered how much longer he would brazen it out. 'Perhaps I should have done that,' Annie said. 'I'm sorry.' She was determined to be friendly towards him. It would encourage his fraud. 'It's all so hazy in my mind,' she said. 'So long ago I can't remember how we met, what we did, where we went.'

Milwaukee smiled with relief. Her amnesia allowed him to invent everything.

'Where did we meet for instance?' she asked.

'In that hospitality party. In the church. I asked you to dance. Don't you remember?'

Annie remembered all right and in a moment of panic she thought he might be true. But then he might well have been in that hall as were so many others who were about to leave for home. 'And after that?' she asked.

'I asked you for a date,' he said, 'and the next day we went walking in the park. I had only a few days left before going home, but we used those days, baby. Oh, did we use those days! Under the trees in the park at night. The moon and the stars. How could you have forgotten?'

Easily, Annie thought, because nothing of the sort had ever happened. She was glad there was no mention of the truck, or the darkness within, or of Ruth or Molly. This was some other Milwaukee, who had decided that Mary was conceived alfresco, under the moon and the stars. She pretended to believe him. She would bide her time. She had first to decide whether she should, with embarrassing proof, disillusion Mary. 'Now I remember,' she said. 'I was young then, and it was beautiful.'

'And you look the same, honey,' he said. 'And it's still beautiful.'

The 'honey' offended her. He was clearly about to make a pass. That was what he had come for. To find somewhere to live, and shamelessly to live with and to live off. 'What are your plans?' she asked. And as if she had read his mind, 'I've nothing to keep me in Milwaukee,' he said. 'I'm divorced and I don't have any children. At least not until now. I worked in a meat-packing plant, but that went kaput.'

It all figured, Annie thought. He had come to London, cunningly paid for, and shamelessly on the sponge. 'How did Mary find you?' she asked.

'She did what you should have done, honey, all those years

ago. She looked up the veterans' register in the City Hall and she rang my apartment bell. I opened the door, and you wouldn't believe this, honey,' he said, 'but the moment I saw her I knew. I knew that she was mine. And she did too, I know. We bonded in that very moment and I can't imagine anything or anybody could pull us apart.'

'So what are your plans?' Annie asked again.

'I'll be honest with you, honey,' he said. 'I'd hoped we could marry and give Mary a loving home. But Mary told me that your marriage seemed happy enough and I'm glad for you. But sad too, honey. Sad for my sake,' he had the nerve to add.

'So what are your plans?' Annie insisted again.

'I'd like to stay for a while,' he said. 'Get to know you all a lot better. I feel I've got some kind of second home here with my daughter and her mother. I made a terrible mistake, honey, but it's not my fault. I didn't know. You didn't tell me.'

'And if I had?' Annie asked.

'I would have come back straightaway. Come back for you, baby. We would have made our home in Milwaukee. We would have been so happy together.'

'I am happy now,' Annie said. She got up from the table. 'I have to help with Freddie's accounts. He has too much work to do. And he earns so much,' she added for Milwaukee's benefit, 'he can't count. And you'd better unpack. I'm sure my mother will help you.'

She found Freddie in their bedroom and, to her dismay, he was packing.

'What are you doing?' she said. She stifled her rising panic. 'Where are you going?' She feared she had already lost him.

'I need to go away,' he said. 'Sort things out. I'll go over to Colin and Clemmie's.'

'But why?' she whispered. 'He's not Milwaukee. He's an imposter.'

'How d'you know? You said you didn't remember what he looked like.'

'I grilled him,' Annie said. 'He got it all wrong. He said we'd gone out together for a week. I only saw Milwaukee the once.'

'And where did you do it?'

She had never before heard a crude Freddie, or witnessed such suppressed anger.

'Where did you do it?' he shouted.

Even Freddie didn't know about the truck. In her shame, Annie had never told him. 'In the park. Under the trees. At least that's what he says.'

'And you don't remember.'

Annie heard the contempt in his voice. 'Freddie,' she pleaded. 'It's almost twenty years ago. He's no more Mary's natural father than you are.'

'Mary doesn't seem to think so,' Freddie said. He pulled violently on the straps of his bag. 'Everything's gone wrong,' he said. 'Nothing will ever be the same again.'

'But even if he is Mary's father, and he can't be, I promise you, but even if he is, why do you have to leave? Nothing need change between us.'

'I don't think Mary will see it that way,' Freddie said. He went to the door. 'I'll be in touch.'

Never had he left the house without kissing her. But now he was gone. She heard the front door slam, something else not in his nature, and she sat on the bed and did not allow herself to cry. She also had to get out of the house. She would have liked to go to Clemmie, but Clemmie had already been claimed. She cursed that it was a Sunday and that there was no teaching to attend to.

But she could not stay in the Freddie-less house any longer. She threw on her coat and she too slammed the front door as she left. Let the conspirators hear that she had done with them. She made her way to the nearest Underground station and bought a ticket for the Circle line. It would suit her, she thought. Suit her indecision, her wavering, her endless self-recrimination, her fear of change. But the Circle line would allow no change. That was its bonus. It was reliable. It would come straight back from where it had started and everything would be as it was before.

She boarded the train at Paddington, and circled giddily for three solid hours, passing the same stations over and over again, while thinking of the home she had left. A safe thought for it denied sequence. Unable and unwilling to move, she anchored her thoughts in the bedroom she had last left. She dared not think further. The train would come full circle and nothing at all would have changed.

When Clemmie arrived at the hospice gates early in the morning, she had to stand aside to let a hearse pass. She panicked. Was it Annie in that box? Bur surely they would have been in touch with her. As soon as the drive was clear, she rushed into reception. 'Who was that?' she almost shouted at an innocent nurse who was arranging flowers.

'Poor Mrs Fox,' the nurse said. 'A lovely lady.'

Clemmie sat down to catch her panicked breath.

'Annie is waiting for you,' she heard the nurse say.

When she had calmed, Clemmie rose and walked slowly down the corridor. She always knew that she would miss Annie, but for the first time she accepted that Annie's absence was a distinct possibility and soon no doubt would be confirmed. She paused again as if to gather courage. And then she saw Mrs Withers coming towards her and she smiled with relief. Mrs Withers was still holding the fort. But, alas, from a wheelchair. She would tell Annie that she had seen her, but she would make no mention of her means of transport. The nurse pulled up the chair to let Clemmie pass.

'Don't take any notice of this,' Mrs Withers was defiant to the last. 'I just thought it would be fun to have a ride,' she said. 'Happened to be a chair spare.'

'Why not?' Clemmie said, smiling.

'I see poor Mrs Fox has gone,' Mrs Withers said, still doggedly in harness. 'Lasted longer than I expected. I'll be up and about tomorrow.' The smile on her face was rigid with effort. 'They'll be needing this chair, no doubt.'

Clemmie laid her hand on her arm. 'I'll tell Annie I saw you.'

'You don't have to mention the chair,' Mrs Withers whispered, and Clemmie could have wept for her.

She found Annie sitting up in bed and nibbling a piece of toast from her breakfast tray. She was relieved to find her friend alert and, as always, welcoming.

'What news, then?' Annie asked as Clemmie sat down. Clemmie was prepared. There was little of change in a daily bulletin, and she had thought long and hard about interesting ways in which she could pass her visiting time. She knew that her friend spent most of her time thinking about her past, dwelling on its sorrows and joys, and she considered that those memories could be more bearable if shared. If brought out into the open, with words exchanged instead of fermenting in the mind without echo. First she told Annie about her meeting with Mrs Withers, who sent her regards.

'Was she in the dining room?' Annie asked.

'She was on her way there,' Clemmie said.

'And how does she look?'

'Well, as always,' Clemmie lied. And as she did so, she prayed that Mrs Withers would hang on, even if wheelchair-bound, until after Annie was no longer anxious for her co-patient's survival.

'What other news?' Annie asked.

Clemmie had no intention of mentioning Mrs Fox. In any case, she didn't think Annie had met her, that she was already bed-bound in Annie's dining-room days. How long ago it seemed, Clemmie thought. And how soon, how sadly soon, would the doctor's prophecy be fulfilled? She tried not to think about it. She opened her bag and brought out a photograph album. 'Last night I was looking through these. My wedding photographs. There's a lovely one of you. Look.' She handed over the right page.

Annie recalled how she had sat in the front pew, on the bride's side of the church, and how she had feared for her friend's union. Colin was clearly no ladies' man. She had guessed at that and so had Freddie. But Clemmie was blinded by love, which shattered all doubts. She had wondered how long it would take Clemmie to understand that she was but a cover for Colin's true self, a cover that would let him pass without sniggers or ridicule.

'D'you remember my wedding?' Clemmie was asking. You didn't have to be dying, she thought, to indulge in recall. You only had to be ageing, because if you were selective, it could be a comfort. What's more, there was often little else to do.

Annie looked at the photograph. It was a threesome. She stood in the middle, between Colin and Freddie, but only she was looking at the camera. Colin's gaze was fixed on Freddie with unveiled adoration, as if his so lately plighted troth to Clemmie had been wrongly addressed. Freddie was grinning with embarrassment.

'You're right,' Annie said. 'It's good of me. It's a happy group,' she felt she had to say.

Then there was a picture of Mary as a bridesmaid. So little, so innocent, so untouched by anger or malice. Annie found it hard to equate that figure with the enraged Milwaukee hunter that it had become.

'These are the reception ones,' Clemmie was saying. She was scanning them herself, and Annie watched her. Clemmie was not smiling. Her face was puzzled. She must be wondering how she could have been so gullible. Yet they had stayed together for fifteen years and when they parted, Clemmie was still a virgin. So there were no custody problems.

'Why didn't I see it?' Clemmie said. 'Or maybe I did but I thought he could change. Still, we had some happy moments. I must count my blessings.'

'No you must not.' Annie was angry. 'No matter how old you are, you are always too young to count your blessings. Counting one's blessings is abdication.' She was glad she had voiced it, for too often in her own recall, she had lingered on blessings and had been tempted to stay with them at the cost of other memories that were less pleasing.

'Here's one of Mary and your mother.' Clemmie handed it over before Annie could refuse. Mary was sitting on her grandmother's lap, and Annie viewed them, both framed in silence and betrayal. 'Things were so different then,' she said.

'Different for me too,' Clemmie said. 'I wish I could blame him. It helps to have someone to blame. But Colin did nothing wrong. He just wanted to be himself and he couldn't help what he was.'

'You're lucky to have no one to blame,' Annie said. 'Blame stunts growth and I want to rid myself of it before I go.'

'Would that help?' Clemmie asked.

'I think so. If I could stop blaming Mary, I could forgive her. And the same goes for her. She must stop blaming me. And while I'm still alive. For her sake, as well as mine. D'you see Mary at all?' Annie asked.

'No,' Clemmie said. 'She's not in touch.' But she was lying. She had seen Mary and had told her of her mother's condition and whereabouts. She had begged her to visit, but Mary had refused. 'You will regret it,' she had told her. 'Perhaps,' Mary had said, and in that response Clemmie had detected a waver, a possibility that she might change her mind. But Annie need not know of that.

'I hear nothing about her,' Clemmie added. 'D'you want me to contact her?' While trying to persuade Mary to visit, she had never been too sure that Annie would welcome her.

'No.' Annie's response was immediate. She had to come of her own free will, and with no persuasion or blackmail. Yet she couldn't bear the thought that she would never see her again. She thought of Mr Fenby who had wanted enough time to live in order to forgive and to be forgiven, but he had been thwarted. 'Tell her to come,' she said suddenly. 'I would like to see her.'

'I'm glad,' Clemmie said, though she dreaded the responsibility of bringing them together. She dreaded that she might fail, fail to grant her friend's last wish. 'I'll be in touch with her,' she said. She began to put the photographs away.

'Leave me the one of Mary. Mary on her own,' Annie said.

Clemmie was pleased with the request and she handed over the photograph. Perhaps its innocence, if it remained in its time, could afford some comfort.

Annie was expecting her solicitor, Mr Lucas, and she needed to rest before he would arrive. So Clemmie took her leave.

'Don't forget,' Annie said, and Clemmie didn't need to ask what she had to remember.

Later that day, Mr Lucas arrived. He had brought with him Annie's will for her perusal and confirmation. It was a simple enough document. Annie had left all her assets to Mary, apart from a generous bequest to Clemmie. She had chosen Mr Lucas, who had already been informed of her wealth, as her executor. Freddie had been generous and had offered her half his salary. But she had refused his offer. She would manage. She was living on her legacy and her teacher's salary had barely been touched during the Freddie years, and had accumulated much interest.

'Are you sure of your bequests?' Mr Lucas asked. 'Read it carefully, then if you're sure, I'll call Matron and a nurse to witness it. Then you don't have to worry about it any more.'

'I never did worry about it,' Annie said. Since being in the hospice she hadn't given it any thought. When she had originally drawn up a will years before, she had balked at Mary being the sole legatee. She had even thought of Battersea Dogs' Home. But she didn't like dogs. Or a children's home. But she was not too sure that she liked children either. She wished that there was a society for the prevention of cruelty to parents and to that she would have given all.

When everything was settled, signed and doubly witnessed, Mr Lucas took his leave. At the door he paused. He felt he should say something but nothing seemed appropriate. 'I wish you better,' he said at last, which meant nothing at all.

Annie smiled her farewell. Perhaps by 'better' he had meant that she could discard recall, or that Mary would come. Either of those would be better than her present state. She felt close to self-pity and she knew that that was not an indulgence to nurture. She reached for her jigsaw. There was still much to be fitted in. She would give Death time in the hope that Death would do the same for her. That's only fair, she said to herself. Death was entitled to reap unfinished business, and did so all the time, but surely a paltry puzzle would qualify for exception.

Mary had noticed Freddie's absence immediately. His chair was empty at the breakfast table.

'Where's Freddie?' she asked.

'He's on tour,' Annie said.

'Not until next week,' Mrs Dawson corrected her.

Annie noticed a sly smile on Mary's face. 'Well, we don't need two fathers in one house,' she said.

'Don't you dare say that,' Annie shouted. 'Freddie has been a wonderful father to you all your life.'

Mary said nothing, but she held her smile.

A whole week had passed since Freddie had left and there had been no word from him. Annie feared he might already have left on his European tour. She didn't want to phone Clemmie. She was too proud. But then, mercifully, Clemmie herself phoned.

'I promised Freddie not to be in touch with you,' she apologised, 'but he's just left.'

'Is he on his way home?' Annie asked.

Clemmie heard the fear in her friend's voice. 'He's gone

to Paris,' she said. 'He left about an hour ago. Shall I come over?'

'No.' Annie's voice was hardly a whisper. 'Later perhaps,' she said. 'I'll ring you.' She wanted to get off the phone, to be by herself, to absorb the strong possibility that Freddie was not coming back. She went to their bedroom and sat on his side of the bed, and slowly and with infinite reluctance, she tried to understand him. And as she did so, she grew angry. What right had he to leave her for such paltry reasons? He obviously felt threatened but he knew that she would never see him usurped. But what worried her most of all was that he seemed not to believe her. On her own admission she had forgotten the event and had not even remembered what Milwaukee looked like. How then was she so sure that he was not real? And if she could remember nothing, how could she be so sure that there were no walks or parks or shades of trees? But she'd remembered the truck. Of that she was certain. But the truck had been mentioned to nobody. Shame had stilled her tongue.

She looked out of the window on to the garden and she saw Mary walking arm-in-arm with her dubious Milwaukee. The sight sickened her. She watched as they crossed into the street. Her mother was alone in the annexe. It was time to confront her. To give her what for. Though about 'what for' she was not clear.

The annexe front door was open and its carelessness irritated her. She found her mother in the living room, happily playing patience.

'What are you up to?' Annie asked.

'Patience,' Mrs Dawson said. 'As you see.'

'You know that's not what I mean. What are you up to with Mary?' Since Milwaukee's arrival this was the first opportunity she had taken to see her mother alone. And what she was up to was exactly what Annie wanted to know.

'I'm looking after Mary and her father,' she said.

'He's not her father,' Annie shouted.

'Mary seems to think so.'

'Then she's wrong. He's no more her natural father than is Freddie. He's conning her. You too, it seems. She was a free ride to England and what it might lead to.'

'What makes you so sure?' Mrs Dawson asked. She did not interrupt her laying down of cards.

'I've questioned him,' Annie said. 'About how we met. Where we went. He got it all wrong.'

'How d'you know?' her mother asked. 'You keep saying you don't remember any of it. Not even what he looked like. If you don't remember anything, how do you know what he says is wrong?'

'Because he was wrong about the only thing I *do* remember.'

'And what was that?' her mother said with contempt.

The word would have to come out. And her mother, her cold, conspiring mother would have to hear it. 'He didn't mention the truck,' Annie said. 'We fucked in the back of an army truck,' she shouted, 'and he didn't mention it. Now are you satisfied?'

Mrs Dawson's nostrils flared with disgust and she spat on the cards on the table.

'Yes. That part I remember.' Annie would not spare her. 'That's where Mary happened. At the back of a filthy army truck.'

Her mother stared at her. 'Slut,' she whispered. 'Of course he wouldn't mention it. He didn't want to shame you.'

'He was there too, you know,' Annie said feebly. She feared

that there might be some truth in what her mother had said. And that there *were* walks and parks and trees and shades. And the truck, that he'd had the decency not to recall.

'A truck,' her mother muttered. 'I'm glad your father's not alive to hear it.'

'So am I,' Annie said, without lowering her voice. 'I'm glad he's dead anyway.'

She left the annexe in a state of tormenting confusion. Supposing her mother was right. That the invader was the true Milwaukee, that he was, in fact, Mary's father. So what? she asked herself. It doesn't matter. Whoever he is, he is not my husband. That word unnerved her. Freddie had to come back, she told herself. They'd been together for so long. He couldn't negate such history. He will come back, she insisted. He would have sorted things out and they could go on together as before. But she could barely convince herself.

The following morning, as they sat around the breakfast table, Annie sneaked the occasional glance at the invader. She was reluctantly open to a new appraisal but she found nothing in his features that suggested a matrix for Mary. And his table manners, unlike Mary's, were rough and greedy. He caught her looking at him and he smiled, but nothing of Mary was reflected in those relaxed features. She did not return his smile. She had concluded without any doubt that the man was a fraud.

'When is Freddie coming back?' Mary asked. 'If ever,' she added. She too was smiling, a sneer-smile that cut through Annie's heart.

'In about a week,' she said bravely. 'Depends on his agent. When are you going back to Oxford?' Annie wanted to change the subject. And she had to admit to herself that she wanted Mary out of the house. She was finding it hard to tolerate her.

'You'll be rid of me soon enough,' Mary laughed. 'I'm going back this afternoon. Grannie's driving me and Dad's coming for the ride.'

Annie was relieved that she would see the back of her, but she was disturbed by her company. The conspirators out on a joyride. But at least she would be alone, and Freddie's absence, if it continued, would not be noted and commented on with contempt. And her mother and Milwaukee could breakfast in the annexe. She would insist on it.

The next morning she found herself alone at the breakfast table. Freddie was due back in England, and she wondered where he would spend the night. If away from home, she would know that it was all over. She left the house quickly and stayed at the school long after lessons were finished. She marked all the essays that had been handed in and it was dark when she left the staffroom and made her fearful way home. The lights were on in the annexe, but her own house was dark. Freddie's gone and he's not coming back, she told herself. She didn't turn on the lights. The dark suited her. She called his name into the darkness. He might have been hiding. He used to play that game with her in the old days when Mary was a baby. But the games were over and she was suddenly overwhelmed by a monumental hatred of her mother, she who had started the ball rolling, she with Milwaukee's name and number, she who with a certain pleasure and malice was now keeping the fires burning. She switched on the light in the kitchen and poured herself a large gin. She was not by nature a drinker, so it took little enough to afford her a modicum of calm, and, slowly, a half-oblivion. Shortly she fell asleep, her head slouched on the kitchen table.

She woke into the light and with a raging thirst.

'What are you doing here?' she heard. She knew the voice,

that gentle voice, and she thought that despite the light and the thirst that she was dreaming. She felt a hand on her shoulder, and she looked up. Freddie was standing there. She clasped his hand, still not believing it.

'I'll get us breakfast,' he said.

She watched his movements around the kitchen. Those routine movements of his that she had witnessed most mornings of their marriage. They were comforting and they signalled an unwillingness to refer to any event that had threatened that routine. He didn't want to talk about his absence, and Annie would honour his silence. He was back home and that was enough for both of them.

'How was the tour?' she asked, as he poured the coffee.

'Good,' he said. 'Paris was wonderful,' he said. 'Next time you must come with me.'

'You forget I have a job,' she laughed.

'How d'you fancy a cruise, then?'

'Where?'

'To America. Two gigs on board. Then a flight home. We could spend a few days in New York. A second honeymoon.'

Oh, he was back. He was back, Annie thought. Her mother could go to hell and take Milwaukee with her.

'It has to be in the school holidays,' she said.

'I can choose my time,' he said. 'Easter perhaps.'

They rose from the table at the same time and hugged each other.

'Where's Mary?' Freddie asked.

'Gone back to Oxford.'

'And Milwaukee?'

'Sponging off my mother.'

'Then good luck to all of them,' he said.

Annie tripped her way to school. Despite her disturbed night, she was far from sleepy. She taught with renewed energy and only after school was over did she allow herself to daydream of New York and to marvel at the sudden shedding of her despair.

At supper that night, Freddie spoke about Colin.

'He's left, you know. Gone to live with Richard in Banbury.'

'When?' Annie asked. She shared Clemmie's pain.

'About a month ago,' Freddie said. 'Clemmie's on her own.'

And Clemmie had said nothing. Perhaps she too had harboured wishes that he would return, and that if she told nobody then perhaps it had never happened. For a whole week, she had looked after Freddie on her own.

'I must go to her,' Annie said.

'Wait until she tells you. She still can't believe it. Fifteen years they were together. Can't be easy for her.'

'I'm surprised it lasted that long,' Annie said. 'He should never have married her. It just wasn't fair.'

'I think he tried his best,' Freddie said. 'He didn't like what he was, but he couldn't go against his nature.'

'Who's this Richard?' Annie asked.

'He's a potter. A good one I'm told. They met at a gig. Clemmie knew him from way back. She introduced them. Dug her own grave, as it were.'

'What's Colin going to do in Banbury?'

'He'll teach. Piano, guitar. He'll make a living. And Richard sells very well.'

'What's Clemmie going to live on?' Annie asked.

'Well, she has the house. And a job. And she could let a couple of rooms.'

Annie envisaged Clemmie's future. And it was dark. 'Did you know this was going to happen?' she asked him.

'No. He said nothing to me. It came as a surprise. I think I ought to go and see him. Though there's nothing I can do. I just have to show him my support. It's nobody's fault. He tried. And it's not Clemmie's fault either.'

The following day Freddie went to visit Colin. When he had gone, Annie dialled Clemmie's number, but it was engaged. She waited and then her own phone rang. Clemmie had been trying to reach her. 'Freddie's back, isn't he,' she said. Then after a pause, 'Can I come over?'

'I'll put the kettle on,' Annie said.

Clemmie did not live far away and within a little while she was standing on the doorstep, dishevelled, tearful and broken.

'I know,' Annie said. 'Freddie told me.' She put her arms around her friend and led her into the kitchen. 'Cry it out,' she said. 'It helps. A bit, anyway.'

'Fifteen years,' Clemmie was saying between sobs. Then she wiped her eyes and swallowed her tears. 'Fifteen years, Annie,' she said again. 'I'm not far off forty and I'm still a virgin.'

So Colin hadn't tried after all, Annie thought.

'He did his best. I thought that given time he'd change. I thought we might even start a family. I was so stupid. I didn't talk to you about it. I was too ashamed.'

Annie decided against the coffee. Instead she poured Clemmie a large brandy. 'You weren't stupid,' she said. 'You loved him, and in his own way, Colin loved you. You're still young and you can start a new life.'

'I'm too old for children,' Clemmie said.

Annie thought of Mary and wondered how much of a blessing children were. 'You can live a good life without children,' she said.

'I keep hoping he'll come back.'

'He won't. It's not only you he's left. He's left a lie, and now he's come clean, there's no going back for him. You mustn't hope for that, Clemmie. In time, when the pain eases, you could become good friends. I'm sure Colin would want that.'

But thoughts of the future would not comfort Clemmie. Her pain was in the present, and any hint of hindsight was no consolation. She wanted to change the subject, to a subject that would not entail Colin's name, for each time she mentioned it, the lump enlarged in her throat. 'How's Mary?' she said. 'Freddie told me about Milwaukee. Is he an imposter? Freddie didn't seem too sure.'

That was information that Annie could do without, and once again she was assailed by those doubts that her mother had so cleverly planted. 'Of course he is,' she said, but she knew that she was only trying to convince herself. 'He's here on the sponge. Freddie's pretty famous in the States and Milwaukee must have visions of great wealth and potential if he could pass as Mary's father. I don't know what he hopes for, but he's only on a visitor's permit, so he can't stay for ever.' Suddenly she envisaged the possibility of his return and that he might well take Mary with him. And Mary would certainly be a willing companion. From her grandfather's legacy to her mother, Mary had access to ample funds, which, cleverly invested, were enough to keep her assumed father and herself with ease. Now it was Annie who wanted to change the subject. But with Colin off-limits, and now Freddie, Mary, Milwaukee and her mother, there was little left to talk about. The American cruise crossed Annie's mind, but she didn't want to claim that she had something to look forward to, while her friend could envisage nothing but a dreary future. So they sat silently together for a while, until the silence became embarrassing.

Then Annie suggested a walk. You could walk without talking and the silence was less noticeable. But Clemmie decided to go home. She wanted to sit by the telephone and wait for Colin's voice, or to be in earshot of a key in the door that would announce his return. Despite Annie's advice, she refused to give up hope. Fifteen years could not be so easily negated. She wondered whether it would have been easier if Colin had left her for another woman, and she had to admit that Richard was less of a destroyer since Colin had not left herself, but simply her gender. This thought comforted her a little and slightly raised her unstable self-esteem. She kissed Annie goodbye, but the kiss was cordial rather than affectionate for she sensed a blatant inequality between them. Annie was conscious of it too, and both women hoped that it would pass else it could well lead to envy, and the erosion of a valued friendship.

As she lay in her bed, Annie thought about her last recall. And when Clemmie arrived on her morning visit, she wondered whether her friend had ever reconciled herself to Colin's desertion. But Clemmie wore her usual smile, and Annie remembered that Colin had died some years before and his death had rendered Clemmie a legitimate widow, a status much easier to bear than that of a deserted wife. Colin had died only a few weeks after Richard had left him for a younger potter, and though the doctors diagnosed a heart attack, Clemmie knew that Colin's heart had not been attacked, but broken.

Clemmie sat by Annie's bed and held her hand. Now the frequent silences between them embarrassed neither woman. They were silences that cemented togetherness. Silences that were the music of dying. There was no longer a need for Scrabble or photograph albums. Recall was not dependent on solid reminder. It filtered through the brain with no respect for calendar and, as Annie neared her end, it filtered less, but ran rampant in her mind, and threatened to flood it with the past, the only tense that was now available.

'I wonder how Mrs Withers is doing,' Annie broke the silence.

'I peeped into the dining room,' Clemmie said, 'and there she was eating her breakfast. She was in deep conversation with her neighbour, so I didn't disturb her.' This was all true, but Clemmie did not mention the wheelchair, which now seemed to frame Mrs Withers like a rehearsal for a coffin.

'I'm glad she's still well,' Annie said. She had to be. Any sign of deterioration Annie would have regarded as a betrayal. Again there was silence until Matron put her head round the curtain.

'You have a visitor,' she said, and she wheeled in Mrs Withers, who gave a sizeable wink to Annie and a large conspiratorial smile. She waited for Matron to withdraw.

'Don't be fooled by this chair,' she said cheerily, as she had said to Clemmie on their last meeting. 'Whenever I see a spare one, I leap into it. Then I get wheeled around. It's fun.'

One could not help but admire the woman's courageous duplicity. But Annie took her word for it. She had to. Mrs Withers looked well enough and Clemmie had said she'd been eating. And Annie was as able to ignore the wheelchair as she could disregard the heavy make-up on Mrs Withers' face, the rouged cheeks, the lipstick, and even, at that early hour, the mascara. She convinced herself that Mrs Withers was well and fit. And, moreover, she was having fun. And she didn't mind that Mrs Withers would return to the lounge and report on her own condition to any resident who would listen. 'Annie's not too well. I just saw her,' she would say. 'She looks terrible. Certainly on her way out, I shouldn't wonder.' Annie smiled. Mrs Withers was keeping the home fires burning and the embers would glow long after she herself had ceased to recall. Then perhaps Mrs Withers would leap from her wheelchair and out of the front door, and go hospice-hopping to pastures new.

As Clemmie was no doubt listening for Colin's key in the door, Annie heard Freddie's unlocking. She rushed to meet him, anxious for news of Colin. She half hoped that Colin might have changed his mind and had decided to return for Clemmie's sake, but she knew it was no solution. Colin and Clemmie were finished and should never have started.

Freddie carried a large bunch of bluebells, newly picked. Colin and Richard lived in a cottage that bordered a wood.

'Colin picked them for you,' Freddie said.

Don't think too badly of me, the bouquet seemed to say. It begged for forgiveness. She put the flowers in water, but took little care with their arrangement. She stuck them into a jam-jar, which she hid behind the saucepans in the kitchen. 'Tell me about them,' she said, as she poured wine for them both.

'Colin's a changed man,' Freddie said. 'I've never seen him so happy. And he looks different too. Younger.'

Although Annie didn't blame Colin, she resented his happiness, for in her mind's eye, Clemmie was still sitting by the telephone.

'They've got such a pretty cottage,' Freddie was saying. 'Thatched roof and inglenooks with open fires. The pottery is

an annexe of the cottage. Richard works there and sells from
there too.'

'And what does Colin do?'

'He's already got guitar students and he's saving up to buy a
piano.'

'All fine and dandy,' Annie said. 'Snug and cosy, the two of
them.' She could not disguise her contempt.

'Well, I'm happy for him,' Freddie said. 'It's the first time in
his life that Colin's being himself.'

'At others' cost,' Annie said. 'Clemmie came over this morning.'

'How was she?'

'What d'you expect? Fifteen years of living a lie. And knowing it all the time, it's true. But having it confirmed is painful.
She's still hoping he'll come back.'

'No chance of that, I'm afraid,' Freddie said. 'We'll just have
to keep an eye on her.' He poured himself some more wine.

Unlike him, Annie thought, and she wondered what more he
had to tell. He took a large gulp and Annie sensed a confession
in the air.

'I saw Mary,' he said.

'Where? How?'

'I was driving back to London and I passed a sign to Oxford.
It was only a few miles so I thought I'd take the chance of
seeing her.'

'Yes?'

'She was in college. Alone in her room.'

'Was she pleased to see you?'

'Surprised. A bit cool at first. I suggested I take her out for
supper. She thought that was a reasonable idea but she stipu-
lated that we weren't to talk about Milwaukee. She made that a

condition. I didn't argue. I was relieved in a way, and we went to a little French bistro that had just opened on the High Street.'

'So what did you talk about? And how was she?'

'She looks good. She seems happy enough. We talked about her work and what she's going to do when she graduates. She mentioned going to live in America, and then she changed the subject, because it threatened Milwaukee. Forbidden territory. Then I took her back to college. She said she had revision to do.'

'Did she mention me?' Annie dared to ask.

'No,' Freddie said. He would not lie to her.

'But she agreed to go out with you.' She clutched at the only hope of the evening.

'Yes,' Freddie said, 'but I sensed a certain reluctance. Between you and me, I was glad she wanted an early night.'

Well, he had tried, Annie thought, but his mention of Mary's American thoughts disturbed her. If only she could prove to Mary that Milwaukee was a fraud, her transatlantic intents would be pointless. And how could she convince Mary if she herself was not convinced? Her mother and even Freddie had stressed her amnesia regarding the whole encounter and she began to wonder whether that amnesia was a protective defence and that the truck was not the only thing there was to remember.

'Can you give me your end-of-term dates?' Freddie interrupted her thoughts. 'I need to arrange the cruise,' he said. 'You do want to come, don't you?'

'Of course,' Annie said. 'I'm excited about it.' But in truth, she was nervous of going away. She was afraid of what might happen when her back was turned. That she would come back

and find Milwaukee gone, together with Mary, and her mother
in the annexe, inscrutable, and playing patience. But she would
not voice these fears to Freddie. It would invite a Milwaukee
discussion and Freddie had made it plain that he did not trust
her unreliable memory.

She slept fitfully that night, and was glad that the following
day was a Saturday and she wouldn't have to go to school. But
she needed to get out. A new supermarket had opened near by.
She would shop for food, not that it was needed, but it was an
excuse to wander, to watch, and to lean on an empty trolley and
relax. And, with luck, take her mind off Milwaukee.

She took a large trolley, family size, though with only two
people to feed, it was hardly warranted. But a paltry basket was
a signal of shopping for one, and though it might have been
more appropriate, it seemed an ill-omen, for she could not rid
herself of the fear that Freddie would leave. He had done it
once, after all, and she feared it might well have been a rehearsal.
It's true he had returned, but her confidence had been shaken.

She wandered around the shelves but found nothing that she
needed. But she couldn't pass through check-out with an empty
trolley. So she bypassed all the edibles and loitered in the clean-
ing section. She could always use washing-up and dishwasher
powder, furniture polish and scourers, kitchen and toilet rolls,
soaps and wipers, until her full trolley reflected an anal obsession
with cleanliness, which was misleading for Annie was far from
house-proud. The thought crossed her mind to shop for her
mother, and with a certain pleasure she ignored it. Let her do
her own shopping, and with her own money. Or send
Milwaukee to the shops to buy whatever he fancied. That
Milwaukee again. She cursed him. Had he not happened, true
or false, everything would have been as it was before. A

contented Mary would have graduated with full honours and she and Freddie would have lived happily ever after. But now all that was threatened and no amount of scouring materials could wipe the slate clean. She dragged her trolley to the check-out point, disgusted with its contents.

In front of her in the waiting line was a woman, a single-basket woman, her shoulders hunched with fatigue. From the back of her, 'I've given up' was clearly readable, and confirmed by the contents of her basket. One lamp chop, a small packet of frozen peas, vainly masking a bottle of sweet sherry. Annie looked at the woman's grey unkempt hair and as the woman opened her bag to pay for her shopping, Annie expected a view of a pension book and travel card. But then the woman turned round. Her scarf had caught on the rail and she made to unhook it. Their eyes met and a glimmer of surprised recognition passed between them. And beneath the surprise, a hint of a smile.

'Molly!' Annie shrieked.

'Annie!' shrieked Molly in simultaneous greeting.

Once again Annie was Milwaukee-flooded, what with Molly out of the blue and her own unintended shopping trip, and the truck their common denominator.

'Time for a coffee?' Annie asked.

'I'll wait for you,' Molly said. She looked suddenly younger and totally at odds with the back view Annie had first encountered.

They found a coffee shop in the shopping precinct. Both women had much to say to each other, but they saved it in silence until their coffees were served.

'You remember the truck?' Annie almost whispered. There was nothing else she wanted to talk about. Perhaps Molly would know more about Milwaukee than she did. It was not possible to know less.

'I try not to think about it,' Molly said, 'but in all these years I haven't been able to get it off my mind. I didn't go to university, although I had a place. I had a sort of breakdown. Nobody understood it. Except me, of course. It was the truck, and I couldn't tell anybody.'

Annie reached out and held her hand. 'I had a baby, you know, from that truck.'

'I'm sorry,' Molly said.

'Don't be sorry,' Annie told her. 'I have a daughter. Mary. She's almost twenty now.'

The tears welled in Molly's eyes. 'It ruined my life, that truck,' she said, and the lamb chop and the frozen peas and the sweet sherry were clear testimonies of her loneliness and despair.

'I've not been with a man since,' she said. 'I try not to think about it.'

Annie held on to her hand. 'You can talk to me about it,' she said. 'I couldn't tell anybody either. But it helps to talk. It would help me too. I don't remember it very well. The details, I mean. I just remember the truck and the darkness inside.'

'I can remember it all,' Molly said. 'You're lucky you've forgotten.'

'I'm not lucky,' Annie said. 'I wish I could recall every second. Every second since we danced in that hall.'

'A foxtrot it was,' Molly said. 'I remember the tune.' And then she set out to prove it. Her voice was off-key, an old-age voice, trembling, but the melody was recognisable and it shipped Annie back on to that dance floor, with its slow, slow, quick quick slow, but with no memory of her partner.

'What else d'you remember?' Annie asked. She was aware

that she was putting herself at risk, at the risk, with Molly's help, of total recall. But it might lead to the discovery of the truth about Milwaukee. Poor Molly. Since that truck her life had been haunted and destroyed by its memory, orchestrated to the foxtrot rhythm. 'It helps to talk about it,' she said again. 'What else do you remember?'

'There were three of them,' she said. 'Don't you even remember that? And they came across to us altogether. Then we danced. They took us in turns. We danced with each of them. They all said they were from Milwaukee. That's in Wisconsin,' Molly added, as if the knowledge of its region would repair her virginity. 'I looked it up in my atlas at home.'

'I don't remember anything of that,' Annie said. 'I can't even remember what mine looked like.'

'I would know him,' Molly volunteered suddenly. 'I danced with him before you did. Before he took you to the truck. He had a tattoo on his wrist. It looked like a bird. I remember not liking it.'

Annie could have hugged her. 'Are you sure this was the one I went with?'

'Yes, I'm sure,' Molly said. 'I followed you. Or rather, I was dragged. By my Milwaukee. Like you were. Then Ruth was behind us. She was the last to be pushed into the truck. We were all laughing, I remember. Like it was a game.'

Annie recalled Ruth for the first time. 'How is Ruth?' she asked.

'She died,' Molly said. 'About ten years ago. She went to university, but she dropped out after a few weeks. Then she got married. To a bookie. She treated him like dirt. She seemed to enjoy it. They broke up after a few months. She kept on having affairs, one-night stands, sleeping with anyone she could find,

and hating them all. Then I heard she'd taken to drink. Poor
Ruth. When she died, they tried to hush it up. Her parents, that
is. They said it was a sudden heart attack. But everybody knew
she'd committed suicide.'

'She died of the truck,' Annie said.

Molly squeezed Annie's hand. 'Let's meet again,' she almost
pleaded.

'Of course we shall. And often,' Annie said. And meant it.
Molly needed support. She recapped on what the three of them
had harvested from that darkness. For herself, she had reaped
Mary; for Molly, a sad abdication, laced with sweet sherry; and
for poor Ruth, a rampage of coital punishment, followed by a
quiet but violent farewell. And her rage against Milwaukee, tat-
tooed or not, and against all the Milwaukees and the trucks that
had housed their infamy, that rage was sublime, and she rose
and hugged Molly to herself, perhaps to infect her with her
own fury, a fury that would dilute her friend's abject resignation, so that she might start living again.

'Poor Ruth,' she said. 'But we must not be beaten, you and
I.' But Annie felt already triumphant. She had not noticed a
tattoo on Milwaukee's wrist. All she had to do was to verify its
absence.

They parted, with arrangements to meet again soon. Annie
walked home. She found herself whistling Molly's recalled
melody. And though its associations were unpleasant, her
whistling was jolly, for she felt she had nailed Milwaukee once
and for all.

As she walked up the drive of the house, she saw him coming
towards her.

'I'm off to Oxford,' he called. 'Taking Mary out to lunch.'

'Mary taking you, more likely,' Annie said.

He ignored her comment and offered to carry her bags to the house, an offer which she refused. Instead, she stopped, put the bags on the ground, then, facing him, she asked him to show her his wrists. She owed him no preamble or courtesy. In her voice was a tone of command.

'Why?' he asked, as he was certainly entitled to.

'Just let me see them,' Annie said.

'You're crazy,' he laughed.

'Just do it,' she shouted at him.

He lifted his arms and Annie swore she smelt his fear. 'Lift up your sleeves,' she said.

His hands were trembling, and loath as she was to touch him, she pushed up his sleeves. Both his wrists were virgin, and with no trace of the scars of erasure.

'Thank you,' she said with a certain satisfaction. 'You are not Mary's father, and you know it.'

'You're crazy,' was his immediate response. 'You've got no proof.'

'Mary's father had a tattoo on his wrist. A bird. I remember it.'

'You made that up, lady,' he said, angry. 'You said you could-n't remember anything. Now suddenly there's a tattoo.' He forced a laugh, but he clearly did not find it funny. In truth, he couldn't hide his anger.

'Since you're into remembering,' he said, 'd'you happen to remember the truck as well?'

The word stunned her and she wondered where he had found it.

'I've not forgotten it,' he went on, 'but I was too ashamed to remind you.'

He was quoting her mother, Annie decided, that vicious

meddler who had prompted him with his lines. Yet she couldn't be too sure, and the old nagging doubts surfaced once again.

'Try to remember the back of the truck,' he said again. 'I can't believe, honey, that you have conveniently forgotten where our daughter started. Picture the truck, honey, and then tell me I'm not Mary's father.' He made to leave. 'I'll tell Mary what you said,' he called back as he walked down the drive. 'I reckon she won't be too happy.' It was a threat and Annie felt that everything was closing in on her. Despite Molly's testimony, she remained uncertain. But what difference did it make after all, she told herself. Whether or not he was Mary's father need have nothing to do with her. And whether or not Mary believed in him was not her business either. Whatever the scenario, she and Freddie were untouchable. 'Bugger them all,' she shouted to herself. She was strangely comforted by such resignation and she hoped that those feelings would last.

She heard Freddie's car slowing up behind her on the drive.

'I've got the cruise brochure,' he called through the open window. 'It's all arranged. Come and look.' He parked the car and took her packages. He peeked inside. 'Are we having a spring clean, then?' he laughed.

He was in a good mood and Annie gladly joined him. Once in the house, she made coffee and they sat around the kitchen table, studying the promising pictures.

'We'll have lots of time to ourselves,' he said. 'And three whole days in New York. How about that?'

She hugged him and 'Bugger Milwaukee' she said to herself again.

'You've got a week to pack,' he said, but Annie wanted to start right away. She was anxious to leave all her doubts behind her. 'I wish we were going tomorrow,' she said. She rushed

upstairs to their bedroom and reached for the holdall that would
serve as hand luggage. It was like a dream, and as she opened
her eyes, she saw that same holdall on the floor, with Clemmie
sitting at her bedside holding her hand.

'Have you been here long?' Annie asked.

'A little while,' Clemmie said. 'You dozed off. But only for a
few minutes. You were talking in your sleep.'

'What was I saying?'

'I couldn't make it out. Except you kept on saying, bugger,
bugger.'

'What's the time?' Annie asked.

'Eight thirty.'

It was morning and Clemmie had only just arrived. Yet in that
small interval she had retraced hours and days of torment and
indecision. She worried that she was hurrying with her recall,
that her whole life, every event of it, would be fully recorded
while she still had time on her dying hands. But how did one
decelerate memory? Except by dissembling, or ornamentation,
and even wishful thinking. During the course of her recall, she
had often been tempted into those traps, but in her honesty, she
had dodged them. Wishful thinking was a pursuit to be kept till
the last of her days. But even then she would avoid it, for it
would make for a sad quietus. She wanted to die having recalled
everything and, by some divine grace, unencumbered with
regrets.

Matron tapped on the curtain. 'You have a visitor, Annie,' she
said.

Annie's heart stuttered. She couldn't imagine who her visitor might be. The doctor wasn't due till the afternoon and Clemmie was already installed. She tried not to hope that it would be Mary and in anticipation she primped her hair and smiled. She hid her disappointment when Molly appeared through the curtain. But she was pleased to see her, and surprised, for she had moved some time ago to Brighton.

'I only just heard you were ill,' Molly said. 'Oh, Annie, I'm so sorry.' She crossed to the bedside and took Annie in her arms.

'I'm glad you came,' Annie said. It took courage, she knew, to visit one who had little time to live. And honesty, too, not to pretend otherwise. Clemmie brought an extra chair for Molly to sit on and then the two women kissed each other. They too were friends, and had been since Annie had brought Molly into their circle. Both knew of the Milwaukee connection, and both refrained from uttering his name.

'How is Brighton?' Annie asked.

'It suits me,' Molly said, and indeed it seemed to, for she looked much younger than her years. And very different from the woman Annie had encountered at the check-out so many years ago. Her hair was now a warm chestnut colour and her complexion reflected the sea-breezes and the sun. Yet she seemed ashamed of her rude health and she sat by the bedside, hunched in her coat, her hands twitching on her knees.

'What news on the outside?' Annie asked.

'Fashion is all the papers write about nowadays. They call it the naughty nineties.'

There was a silence then. The naughty nineties was clearly not a subject that would easily get off the ground.

'Bugger what they call them,' Annie shouted, then

straightaway fell into an explosion of sobbing that burst from every part of her failing body.

They let her cry it out. There was nothing they could do or say. Any words of comfort would have been sheer hypocrisy. They couldn't tell her she'd feel better in the morning, or a good sleep was what she needed, for perhaps for her there would be no morning, and a good sleep was her future whether she needed it or not. So they sat there and listened to her offended weeping, her simmering rage and its hot it's-not-fair tears. And as suddenly as she had begun, she stopped, dragged the sheet across her face, attempted a smile and murmured, 'I'm sorry.' And still there were no words to comfort her.

But Clemmie was disturbed. It was the first time in all her weeks of vigil that she had seen her friend break down, and she had to surmise that it was the first public breakdown, but that in private, and alone, in the long endless nights, the unfairness of it all would pierce her heart. There was nothing to say, and nothing to do. Scrabble was now beyond her and the jigsaw, even if she could manage it, was a solitary pursuit. There was nothing to do but wait, and quietly hope that the end would come soon. But not too soon. For Clemmie, like Annie, hoped for Mary's appearance. Such a visit would put things in order, and to rights, and would relieve her friend of her desperate hanging-on, her hopeful waiting. Such a visit would draw a line beneath a life of loving, hating and a craving to forgive. Without such a line, Annie's life would be truly unfinished. Only one life one had, and only one death, and both would be wasted if not somehow fulfilled. Clemmie put her arm around Annie's shoulder and knew no words to utter.

Molly had begun to cry.

'Oh shut up, for God's sake,' Annie said, though not

unkindly, for she was smiling. 'I'm ready to go,' she said. 'Almost.' The word 'Mary' could find no other outlet. 'Almost' was the best she could do.

Clemmie wanted to leave. She wanted to see Mary and if necessary force her to see her mother for the last time. She had never taken to her friend's daughter, even when she was a child. There was a dark side to her, an evil side almost, which had budded as she grew and was now in full flower. She would have to try to hide how much she hated her.

'I need to sleep,' Annie said, and that gave both of her visitors permission to leave. Molly was still crying and her tears rinsed Annie's face as she kissed her goodbye. But Clemmie did not kiss her friend. She would be back very soon, she decided, and with Mary, and, if necessary, with a gun in her back.

When they had gone, Annie was relieved to be alone. She didn't want to sleep. There was time enough for that. And though her body ached with weariness, her mind was too active to take a rest. She had to get back to her cruise-packing, and though she now knew that the holdall would not travel, she had to recall why.

With absolute clarity, she viewed the sponge-bag, the make-up case, the box of exquisite jewellery – Freddie's presents over the years – the three novels that would cover the crossing, the Walkman with Freddie's tapes. But clearest of all, she saw the half-closed zipping, with just enough room left for those last-minute forgotten things, things that never had to be remembered. She eyed the holdall on the floor of her cubicle, which now could be terminally zipped, and she found herself back in the dark corridor of memory, half-willingly, but unable to stop herself.

*

She'd gone shopping for those last-minute things, though the cruise was yet a week away. But she was determined to make a production of anticipation, of a looking-forward-to. That was part of the pleasure, of imagining the moonlit nights on the water, the dancing as they did in the beginning in Freddie's unknown days, and, above all, the absence of Mary and her mother, and Milwaukee, and all the chaos that that trio entailed.

It was evening when she returned from shopping, and Freddie was cooking supper. Nothing has changed, she kept saying to herself. Nothing.

Until there was a banging of doors and she felt a furious entry. Calamity throbbed at the kitchen door and she knew it without turning.

'Annie,' she heard Milwaukee's voice. 'Mary's in a state.'

And it was then that she turned around. Mary stood there like a casualty under Milwaukee's arm.

'What's happened?' Annie asked. There was no sign of wounding, no blood, no bandage, and that should have afforded some relief. But from Mary's look and her trembling, there seemed something far worse than a treatable wound. It seemed that her world, however distorted, had collapsed around her.

'What is it?' Annie asked again.

'Go on,' Milwaukee said. 'You tell her.'

'What is it?' Freddie asked gently. 'You can tell us, whatever it is.'

'And you of all people, you damned well ought to know,' Milwaukee shouted.

'What's happened?' Annie screamed. Already she knew and she was afraid.

'He raped her, that's what.'

'Who?' Annie whispered.

Then Mary spoke for the first time. Or rather spat. 'Your husband,' she hissed. 'Yesterday. In my room.'

Annie looked at Freddie for a clue. But he said nothing. He simply walked over to Mary, shoved Milwaukee aside, then slapped her hard across her face. His gesture, Annie feared, could have meant anything. Mary's nose spurted blood, a real wound, and Annie viewed it as a relief. It was something that could be dealt with, for the rest must surely be untreatable. She ran a flannel under the cold-water tap, and handed it to Mary.

'She told me,' Milwaukee was saying. 'She wasn't going to say anything. She didn't want to make trouble. But by God,' he said, full of virtue, 'I thought you, Annie, ought to know.'

'She's lying,' Freddie shouted.

Annie sank into a chair, burdened once again with the great weight of her doubts. Was Milwaukee indeed Mary's father? Was Mary telling the truth? Did Freddie? No. Impossible.

'Freddie says you're lying, Mary,' she said and she wished her voice carried more conviction. 'You're nothing but a trouble-maker. A marriage-breaker. What have we ever done to you?'

'I've told her she should go to the police,' Milwaukee put his oar in.

'That's enough,' Annie said. She rose to stand by Freddie's side. He put his arm around her. But it was not a gentle embrace. It was a grip, defiant, and it could have confirmed either his guilt or his innocence. And, despite herself, Annie already felt Mary's skin on his fingertips, and she shrank from his touch. And in that movement, and at that moment, Freddie knew that their marriage was over. Gone, together with the trust that had maintained it. He turned from her and left the room.

'Can't face it, can he,' Milwaukee said.

Annie ignored him. 'I'd like to speak to Mary. Alone.'

'Mary?' he asked.

'Stay with me,' she said.

Annie felt beaten. 'I want to hear about it,' she said.

'I told you. He came to my room, and he raped me.'

'I don't believe a word of it,' Annie said.

'Because you can't afford to. That's why.'

Then Annie lost her cool. 'Get out,' she said, 'both of you. Tell it to your grannie. It's a proper grandmother's tale.'

'I hope you can live with it,' Mary said. Then she put her arm round Milwaukee's waist and he led her out of the room. At the door she turned. 'You haven't heard the last of this,' she said.

Annie didn't know what to do. And worse, she didn't know what to think. If the story had been a mere performance, based on a vicious lie, then it had certainly been well rehearsed. Mary, in her schooldays, had often shown acting talent, and her performance had been convincing enough. But if it were all a lie, what was its motive? And if the truth – she dared not think about that. She knew she should go straight to Freddie. But she didn't know what to say to him. He surely knew that she suspected him, that she suspected Mary was telling the truth. Her shiver at his touch had not gone unnoticed. But if she did not seek him out, he would assume that she believed every word of Mary's story. She rushed to the living room. But it was empty. Then up to their bedroom. Empty too. She called his name loudly through the house, and was slapped in the face by an empty echo. He's left, she thought. Back in the bedroom she opened his wardrobe and was relieved to find his clothes *in situ*.

And his toothbrush and shaver in the bathroom. Through the window she saw that his car was in the driveway. He must have gone for a walk, she decided. Or perhaps he had gone to the annexe and vented his spleen more precisely. Then she spotted him, leaning against the oak tree in the drive, his back towards her, and his head hung low. There was no movement in him, and his stillness frightened her. She ran out of the house and, still with no notion of what to say, joined him at the tree and reached for his hand. It lay limp and unresponsive in hers.

'You believe her, don't you,' he said. 'Don't deny it.'

'I want to hear it from you,' Annie said. 'I want you to tell me it isn't true.'

'How could you dream it was true? How could it even cross your mind?'

'It didn't,' Annie lied. 'I just want to hear it from *you*.'

'And if I deny it, would you believe me?' he asked. 'Without any proof?'

She would not lie to him. 'I don't know,' she said. 'I don't know what to think any more.'

Then he put his arms around her, and whispered in her ear. She remembered how, years ago, the day that they had moved into the house, they had stood together on that same spot, and in a similar embrace, and he had whispered in her ear, 'I love you.' Now, in that same place, and in that same ear, he whispered, 'It's over.'

As he loosened his arms, their imprint ignited a lightning strike through her whole body. She turned and watched him walk back towards the house. She leant against the tree and felt the warmth of his body that still lingered on the trunk, and the doubts that had hitherto trickled through her veins now flooded her entire. He had not confessed to rape. Neither had he denied it. But she knew it wasn't a deliberate tease. He simply didn't trust her any more. Her doubts had triggered that mistrust. They were enough to draw a line between them. They were enough to merit his parting words, 'It's over.' She knew that there was no point now in trying to dissuade him, and she knew too that she would never know whether or not Mary had been telling the truth.

She stayed leaning against the tree for a long while. She knew she had to fight, but with what weapon? She would plead their history together and the folly of negating all those years. But history was a paltry weapon then faced with his armoury of mistrust. She had lost him, she knew. This time, he would not come back. And as if to confirm it, she heard his car revving behind her. She watched it pass down the drive and noted the laden luggage-rack on the roof. She noted his face too, grim and determined, yet unable to hide the traces of sorrow.

She watched the car out of the drive and then she returned to the house and to their bedroom to view the hollow he had left behind. There was no sign of hurried packing. The room was tidy and it was not until she opened the drawers and wardrobe that she found any sign of change. The empty spaces with no hint of what had once filled them. No stray button, not a single sock, not a single proof even of gender. She went into their bathroom and smelt the traces of him in the aftershave lotion that he had spilt in his hurried departure. Soon that too would evaporate and all that would be left of him would be his heart-piercing absence. She looked at what was left on the shelves, the perfumes he had bought her, the anti-ageing creams of which he had disapproved, the lotions, lipsticks, mascara, eye-shadows, all the artefacts with which she hoped to keep him by her side, though she knew she could have kept him without any of them.

With one swift movement of her arm, she scooped them all into the waste bin. Pretences, all of them. She had denied him trust, and that was why he had gone.

She went back into the bedroom and sat on the edge of the bed. Gingerly and on the side where he slept. At her feet she saw the half-zipped holdall, that luggage that now would never cruise, and she raced back to the hospice for sanctuary.

Clemmie squeezed her hand and Annie opened her eyes. 'What day is it?' she asked. It was her oblique method of finding out how much time she had left. Clemmie lied about the date, giving her a month longer than the doctor had prescribed. Annie knew only that time was passing but she had no notion of its divisions into night and day. Clemmie thought that her friend might be close to coma, but her voice was still strong, sometimes hesitant, as if looking for words, but then finding them, and once again strong.

'Did I talk in my sleep again?' she asked.

'No,' Clemmie said. She had been struck by the silence of her friend's slumber. And by the seeming peace of it. 'You were very quiet,' Clemmie said. 'I suppose you had a pleasant dream.'

There was no logic in that, Annie thought. She remembered how, in her teens, in her belt-non-buckling days, she had suffered dreadful nightmares, yet in the morning she had marvelled at her unruffled bed, her uncreased sheets, and smooth pillows. The bed did not translate the dream any more than her silent, peaceful slumber reflected the horror of her recall. 'Freddie left me,' she said.

But that was many years ago, Clemmie thought. Her friend

had a long way to travel in her recall and she feared that there would not be enough time for Annie to close the circle.

And as if Annie were reading her thoughts, she said, 'Years and years can be remembered in a blink of an eye. It's those moments of truth or lies, or betrayals or love, it's those moments that demand the extended recall. I wondered where he'd gone,' she said. 'I knew he'd go on the cruise and, foolishly I suppose, I expected a card from him. But nothing came. For weeks I ran to collect the post. But nothing. It was as if he had never been. And he didn't write to you either,' she said.

'No,' Clemmie answered, and she was telling the truth. Freddie hadn't written. Instead he had visited. She remembered her surprise at seeing him at the door. Her first question before she invited him inside was to ask if Annie knew of his visit. He shook his head. 'No. And I don't want her to know. But I need to see you.'

She asked him inside. She hoped that he wanted to arrange a reconciliation and she welcomed him. But she was faintly unnerved by his radiant manner and his handsome face with its cruise-tan and his sun-bleached hair. He looked far too happy for her peace of mind. So she decided not to offer him coffee in case she might regret her hospitality.

He sat down at the table facing her and smiling. 'I need you as a go-between,' he said.

Again she was hopeful of a reconciliation. 'Between you and Annie? Yes, of course,' she said. 'Anything that would bring you together again. I know she wants it desperately.'

'It's . . . it's not like that,' Freddie stammered.

She began to hate him. Especially his good looks and his radiance. She waited for him to explain himself.

'I'm in love,' he said. 'And I want a divorce.'

Since Colin's desertion, Clemmie hadn't felt too kindly towards the whole male tribe and Freddie of all men had turned out like the rest of them. 'You didn't lose much time,' she said with contempt.

'I couldn't help myself,' he said. 'Her name's Alison. She was on the cruise and we met—'

Clemmie stood up, interrupting him. 'I don't want to hear anything about her,' she said. 'You've not come here for my help. You've come here to show off. You've come here to let me know that you can still make it. I want you to get out, and I don't want to see you again.' And she practically shoved him out of the door.

She hadn't told Annie about that meeting, and never would, even now as she pressed her friend's dying hand. Annie was right. Some recall required but a blink of an eye, and she shuddered at the memory.

Annie had dozed off again. The doctor drew the curtain and crossed to Annie's bed.

'You're a good friend,' he said to Clemmie. 'How has she been?' he asked, taking Annie's hand.

'In and out of sleep,' Clemmie said.

'And her mind?'

'Lucid still.'

'Keep talking to her if you can,' he said. 'She will hear everything. Hearing is the last sense to go.'

But that was not what Clemmie intended to do. She knew of Annie's backward and detoured journey and she would not interrupt it with her comments. Annie needed others' silence for that journey, and Clemmie could only hold her hand on her precarious way.

*

Annie would not tell Mary of Freddie's desertion. She did not want to witness her pleasure. In any case she would find out soon enough. She didn't know what to do with herself. She knew that this was no time to make a radical decision. But there would be no harm in writing to him. She could send a letter, care of his agent, for she didn't know Freddie's whereabouts. She would swear that she had never doubted him. She would beg him to return. Thus she wrote, and hurriedly, for she wanted to lose no time in reaching him. Now there was nothing more that she could do except to go about her business and wait for the post.

And so, for that first week, she went to school and to the postbox on her way, and then she had to face the Easter holiday that should have been spent at sea. It was a difficult time. She had not seen Mary or Milwaukee or even her mother since the day of the accusation. It seemed that they were avoiding the house. Surely by now they must have noticed that Freddie's car was gone. And surely they had seen her leave the house in the days when she should have been at sea. They knew. Of that she was convinced. In time they would find an excuse to visit, simply to confirm what they suspected, and possibly welcomed.

And one day, on a Sunday, when Freddie's car had been absent for over a month, Annie's mother came through the kitchen door. Annie surprised herself at being glad to see her. Despite the eternal friction between them, she retained a certain affection for her mother, which was due to nothing else but nature. For her mother had given her little loving in her time, and a faintly grudging care. She invited her to sit down, and she put the kettle on for tea.

'Nothing for me,' her mother said. 'I've just had breakfast.' It seemed a hostile beginning. Mrs Dawson wanted no favours. She had come simply for information. 'What's going on?' she said.

'You tell me,' Annie suggested. 'You probably know more than I do.'

'Where's Freddie?' Mrs Dawson came straight to the point.

And so did Annie. 'He's gone,' she said. 'He's left me.' For the first time since Freddie's departure, Annie believed it. She had said it aloud. It was true. He was not coming back. And there would be no post. She started to cry, shrinking her body, pre-empting a possible touch of consolation. But she needn't have bothered. Mrs Dawson didn't move.

'I'm not surprised,' she said. 'How could he stay here after what he did?'

'I'm not sure he did anything,' Annie said.

'Are you calling your own daughter a liar? What reason would she have to invent such a terrible story?'

'Oh, I could think of lots of reasons,' Annie said. 'Revenge perhaps? Wanted to get rid of Freddie? Tell her he's gone. That should please her.'

'Revenge?' Mrs Dawson said. 'For what? And why should she want Freddie to go? The poor girl's in a terrible state.'

Her mother was right, Annie thought, and the possibility that Mary had spoken the truth now seemed more and more acceptable. She recalled Freddie's return from Oxford and his description of his Mary encounter. He had seemed nervous, hesitant. But it was too early to forgive Mary, too early to embrace her. Too early to apologise. She needed to cling to her doubts. Without those, she would have to bury Freddie once and for all.

'I would never have thought it possible,' her mother was

saying. 'Mind you, I often caught him looking at her. In a kind of leery way. And he cuddled her a lot. It used to worry me.'

'He loved her, that's all,' Annie said. 'I think Milwaukee put her up to it. They'd rehearsed it, both of them.'

'Why should a father want to use his child like that?' Mrs Dawson was horrified.

'He's not her father. I keep telling you.'

'You've no proof of that. Except your unreliable memory. In any case, Mary is convinced he is her father and that's all that matters.'

There was no point in arguing with her.

'What are you going to do?' her mother asked.

'You seem to know all the answers,' Annie said. Her comfortable irritation with her mother had loyally surfaced.

'You must get a divorce,' she said. 'Marry again.'

Annie laughed. 'And I'm sure you have someone in mind.'

'You could do worse,' Mrs Dawson said. She rose to leave. She had got what she had come for and she would carry her news back to the annexe.

Annie did not want to think about what had happened but she knew it was time to consider the future. Her mother's suggestion of divorce was characteristically cruel. It denied her any hope of Freddie's return. In any case, she did not know where he was. She would go on waiting for the post, she decided, and wondered how long she would allow for the waiting. Nowadays she would pass the postbox at the end of the drive without looking inside. She would tease herself with as much as three days' disregard in the hope that Freddie was waiting for her back to be turned. But still there was nothing and she wished she could give up hope. In her daily meetings with Clemmie, she listened as her friend tried to persuade her to forget him, to

give herself a new chance in life. But Annie thought there
should be somebody who went on hoping. She could not abandon Freddie. She would give him another week, she decided.

But that week stretched to a month and still there was no
post. She threw herself into her work. She volunteered for extra
teaching duties. Every evening she dreaded the return to the
empty house. She calculated the time that had passed since
Freddie had left. At first she had reckoned in hours, then in
days. Slowly it became weeks, and as hope became harder to
hold on to, her reckoning was monthly. It was long enough, she
told herself. It was time to vent her anger, an anger that might
lead to hate. And that would be good too, as long as she didn't
allow it to lead to bitterness. It would help me to hate him, she
said to herself.

It was dark as she reached the driveway and, turning, she
stroked the postbox, which she hadn't opened for a week. She
lifted the lid, and blindly felt inside. She clutched at a number of
letters. Bills, she thought, overdue probably, that needed to be
paid. She plucked them out of the box and went to study them
under the lamplight in the street. There were indeed bills, but
Freddie's handwriting on one of the envelopes could not have
signalled an invoice. She trembled with a timid trickle of hope.
She would not have to be angry. She would not have to hate.
She could bypass bitterness, and she could scuttle her despair.
She hurried into the house, trembling.

She poured herself a drink. It would serve for whatever
matter the letter contained. She was nervous of opening it. She
feared it might be a letter of a stranger, long gone from home.
Or it might be a begging letter, a take-me-back letter, an I've-
made-a-terrible-mistake letter. Or it could be an irrevocable
farewell. She poured herself another drink. She considered

postponing the opening until the morning. Any news, good or bad, looked better or less worse in the morning light. But she didn't think she could sleep while the letter lay unopened on the table. She poured herself another drink, as if she wanted to anaesthetise herself against hurtful news. And then another. Then, close to hysteria, she tore the letter open and, as if she needed a witness, she began to read it aloud. 'Dearest,' it said. She did not like that word. It was old-fashioned, dated, and spoke of long ago. It acknowledged a past, but a past that promised no future. She heard a tone of consolation in the word, that bordered on pity. She braced herself to read further.

It's been some time now since we parted, and I've had time to think about what happened between us. At first I thought perhaps we could get together again and I hoped that that would be possible. But now I realise that our marriage is a closed chapter.

Annie put the letter aside. She needed a pause. A pause to give up hope. But a mere pause would not be long enough to abandon the hope she had clung to for so long. Freddie was not coming back. She realised that with all its logical compulsion, but it was a knowledge that would take some time to travel to her heart. She poured herself another drink and when she picked up the letter again, the words, though still readable, were blurred, which seemed to soften the cruelty of their import.

I left you because you no longer trusted me. You were not loyal. And that says it all. I could not remain in a partnership that was coloured with suspicion. It would

have been uncomfortable for both of us. I shall always
remember the happy times we shared and all the good
that you brought to me. My affection for you will not
wane with time, but I think you owe yourself a new life, a
new start, and hopefully with one who is worthy of you.
I want the same for myself. I think it best we apply for a
divorce.

Another drink. Another blurring, so that his last sentences were
almost unreadable through her tears.

I think it better for both of us if we do not meet. Our
solicitors can draw up arrangements and you will shortly
be hearing from mine. I wish you all the best.
    Freddie.

Another drink, and hopefully coma. She laid her head on the
table with barely enough strength to cradle it in her arms for
comfort. Sleep came mercifully soon, and was undisturbed until
the early morning. Though had a witness been present, he
would have shuddered at the curdling groans, loud enough to
wake the sleeper herself. Which they did, but not until the
dawn.

Annie woke slowly, but she needed no time to understand
where she was and why. But first she had to deal with a raging
thirst. A concrete thing. Dealable with. A long and slow drink of
water gave her immense pleasure. Then a splash of cold water
on her face prepared her to deal with the day. Until she realised
the matter to be dealt with.

It was a Saturday so there was no school to use for postponement. And likewise no working solicitor to contact. She

could do nothing except read the letter over and over again to make sure she hadn't simply had a bad dream. She picked up the letter and noticed that its last paragraph had been smudged by her tears. Only the word 'solicitor' was unblurred, but she knew its contents by heart. She folded the letter and put it in her bag. She was going to be sensible. She would take a shower, dress in her smartest, and then, at a reasonable hour, she would call on Clemmie and together they would plan a strategy. For strategy was called for, she thought. No victim's acquiescence, which was the first thought that had crossed her mind. No cordial acceptance. What was required was a fight, an onset of battle, with no respect for decorum or propriety.

In the shower, she built up a storm of rage, which she knew might lead to hatred. But she needed to hate, at least for a time. It would stem her natural inclination to submit, to acquiesce, to avoid making trouble. There had been no mention of Mary in his letter, an omission that struck her with its ambiguity. Had he mentioned her, her name would have entailed confession or denial, demanded it even, and its omission let him off the hook of both. She kept her doubts, but she had to admit to herself that she was veering towards Mary's version as the truth, and that fed her hatred for the man she had once loved. And still did, she screamed aloud, as she pummelled her body under the spouting jets.

She dressed and made herself a substantial breakfast, marvelling at her appetite. Afterwards she rang Clemmie and asked if she could come over. She thought that Clemmie's voice sounded nervous, as if she was hesitant about the visit. Perhaps she had just got up, Annie thought, and her voice was still sleeping. She would give her time to rouse herself, so slowly she took the half-mile walk to Clemmie's house.

Clemmie was welcoming as always, though she wore a worried expression. 'You've heard from him?' she asked, as Annie came through the door.

Annie waved the letter.

Clemmie was nervous. She feared the mention of Alison, that name to which she was privy. Yet her friend did not seem downcast. Rather she had a fighting air about her, almost manic.

'He's a bastard,' Annie shouted. She thrust the letter into Clemmie's hand. 'Read it,' she said, 'and tell me what to do.'

Clemmie put her arms around her. 'Let's have coffee first,' she said.

'I'll make it.' Annie went into the kitchen. 'You read the letter.'

Clemmie was glad to read it unwitnessed, so that no trace of foreknowledge would be visible. She was surprised to hear Annie singing in the kitchen. But it was no glee-song. It sounded like a battlecry. Clemmie heard it as a call to arms, and she picked up the letter to learn the nature of the conflict.

At first, she scanned the lines for a mention of Alison. Not finding any reference, she was relieved and she settled down to read the letter carefully. It struck her as being cold, almost as if it had been dictated by an interested party. She imagined Alison standing at his side, stripping the words of any affection that might be open to misinterpretation. It was a plain epistle, that could not be misread. Unadorned, without nuance, without *double entendre*. It was a take-it-or-leave-it letter and, apart from a few personal references, it might well have been written by a solicitor.

'Bastard,' Clemmie shouted as Annie brought in their coffee. 'What are you going to do?'

'Sit on it for a while.'

'You've had a while,' Clemmie said. 'It was posted over a week ago.' She pointed out the date on the envelope.

'It's been sitting in the postbox,' Annie said. 'I gave up looking for it. Anyway, he says I'll hear from his solicitor. I'll wait for that, and then I'll keep them waiting.' She even gave a smile, and Clemmie joined her.

'We'll give them a run for their money,' Clemmie said.

'What money?' Annie asked, astonished.

'Alimony, for God's sake.'

'I don't need the money. I don't want his money,' Annie said.

Clemmie was angry. 'It's nothing to do with need. He owes you. He walked out on you after all those years. He's damned well got to pay.' No doubt she was thinking of Colin.

'But I don't want to punish him,' Annie said.

'And why not?' Clemmie was exasperated.

Annie smiled, knowing the folly of what she was about to say. 'Because I don't want him to think badly of me,' she said. And she meant it, though she pitied herself for playing the victim.

'Then pay *him*,' Clemmie said with contempt. 'Give him the house and everything in it. Then I suppose he'll think highly of you.' She paused then. 'Annie, for God's sake, don't put yourself down so. You're entitled to half his earnings. At least. And who kept him when he wasn't earning? In the beginning with Colin's combo. You did, with your legacy. He rode your back for years. I wish it were my divorce,' she said. 'I'd take him to the cleaners.'

Annie thought her friend was more angry with Freddie than she was herself and she stretched out her hand, glad of their friendship. 'Drink your coffee,' she said.

For a while they were silent. 'D'you know a solicitor?' Annie asked. 'A fair one.'

'There's no such thing,' Clemmie said. 'They're all out for what they can get. Especially divorce ones.' She spoke as if from experience, though she and Colin had never divorced and, without argument, he had continued to support her.

'I don't know one,' she said. 'But I'll look out for you. But promise me you won't argue with him. You'll take his advice.'

'I promise,' Annie said, though she hardly meant it. But she wanted to avoid argument. 'I have an awful feeling he has another woman,' Annie said out of the blue.

'How would you feel about that?' Clemmie tested the waters.

'I think I would die,' Annie said.

'It could happen though. It usually does. But you could find another man too.'

'I think it's unfair he won't meet me. Could I insist on that, d'you think?' Annie asked. 'Before we come to some agreement. I'm entitled to talk to him.' She was tearful. 'How can he do this to me after so long?'

'It's better this way,' Clemmie said. 'A clean break. It would only hurt you more to see him.'

'I'm beginning to hate him,' Annie said.

'I'm delighted to hear it.' Clemmie put her hand on Annie's arm. 'It means you're recovering.'

The following day Clemmie located a solicitor, one who specialised in divorce. Over the phone she gave his name and particulars to Annie, who wrote them down and put them away with the intention of doing nothing about them, even though, with the morning's post, she had received a letter from Freddie's solicitors. She had heard of them. Their name was notorious in the divorce cases of stars. They were known always to win hands down. Clemmie's find was a pygmy amongst them. She let the letter lie. Its contents offended her. It requested the name and address of the solicitor of her choice. It wished to forward to that said solicitor a copy of a deposition from their client, outlining his arrangements for divorce proceedings. She resented the letter. It put insulting mileage between herself and the man with whom she had been so intimate for so long. The letter intimated a corre-spondence between two total strangers. She put it aside, together with Clemmie's information and she tried to forget about them.

But midweek she received a phonecall from Freddie's body-guards, urging her response. Then the following week a letter arrived from the same source, with vague threats of subpoenas. Tearfully, she picked up the phone and arranged a meeting with her pygmy. He was friendly and consoling. He promised to contact the giants and request their deposition. He arranged a meeting with her early the following week. He told her he'd do his best for her. But all Annie knew was that what was best for her could not be granted by any solicitor. She said nothing of the meeting to Clemmie. She feared her legal advice, her take-him-to-the-cleaners advice, which it wasn't in her nature to follow.

The meeting was arranged for midweek after school. She arrived in his office in her unsmart working clothes. She made no concessions. She felt she was there as a witness, a witness to somebody else's breakdown of marriage. It had nothing to do with her and her Freddie, and as long as she could pose as a wit-ness, she would survive the interview.

His name was Mr Tweedie, and he was, appropriately, a tweedy sort of person. His clothes were of that material. He smoked a pipe, and Annie thought he probably wore a deer-stalker. He was a small-time Sherlock Holmes, which suited his calling. He offered her a cup of coffee, which he himself dispensed from a machine in the corner.

'Now let's get down to it,' he said.

'What d'you want me to say?' she asked, still as a witness, willing to help the case along.

'Nothing at the moment,' Mr Tweedie said. 'Just listen. I'll read you out the deposition from your husband.'

'*My* husband?' she asked. Her role as witness was threatened.

'Of course,' Mr Tweedie said. 'Mr Freddie Morgan.' He wondered whether his client was deranged. He noted her crest-fallen look. He opened a side drawer in his desk and drew out a half-full bottle of whisky together with a paper cup. He poured a small measure. 'Perhaps this will help,' he said, handing her a cup.

Annie took it gratefully and swallowed the liquid in one gulp. 'Thank you,' she said. She knew she could no longer play the witness. It was face-the-music time. 'You were talking about my husband,' she said.

He handed the papers to her. 'Would you like to read it?' he asked.

'You read it to me,' she said. If it were read aloud, and by a disinterested party, she would have to believe the words whatever their matter.

'I'll leave out the legal jargon,' Mr Tweedie said kindly. 'I'll just give you the gist.' He put on his horn-rimmed spectacles and started to read. 'Basically,' he said, 'your husband is asking for a divorce, and he is offering as grounds his adultery.'

'Pardon?' Annie whispered. 'Is he inventing those grounds?'

'No,' Mr Tweedie said. 'He has given a name and there is

confirmation.' He noticed how she trembled and tried to hold back the tears. He reached once more for the bottle and refilled her cup. Blindly she picked it up and drank it quickly, spilling a little down her chin.

'What's her name?' she asked. She would buy a gun, she decided, seek her out, and kill her. Or better, a knife; that would ensure a slower death and one that was infinitely more painful. 'What's her name?' she almost screamed at her pygmy.

'Alison,' he said. 'Alison Bates.'

'And where does she live?'

'The address is not given.'

'And where does my husband live?' She could no longer utter his name.

'His solicitors are not obliged to divulge his whereabouts.'

She felt utterly beaten. Humiliated. Diminished. But not by Freddie. Her rage stormed around that Alison. It was all her fault. It was she who had broken up her marriage. Freddie was not culpable. Now she made no attempt to hold back her tears. Mr Tweedie passed a box of tissues across his desk, eyed his shrinking bottle, and refilled her cup. Then after a second's pause, he decided that he too needed a measure of support and he took a generous swig direct from the bottle. 'Shall I go on?' he asked.

Annie nodded. The worst was over. There could be nothing on earth worse than Alison.

'Now we come to the settlement,' Mr Tweedie said. He hummed a paragraph of legal jargon, then, 'Basically, he's offering you the house, apart from the annexe, the deeds of which he wishes to be put in his stepdaughter's name. Mary Dawson.'

Mr Tweedie looked up to see the effect of that offer on his client. He found it odd that she was smiling, and odder too that she burst into laughter. He did not enquire as to the reason for her sudden change. He thought he preferred not to know. But Annie herself didn't know why she was laughing. She knew it was certainly not from pleasure. Rather from bewilderment and the re-emergence of her doubts. Did the legacy confirm that Freddie had raped Mary and that the annexe was by way of a consolation prize? Or was it rather a confirmation of his own innocence?

Mr Tweedie let the laughter subside. 'Shall I go on?' he said.

She wondered who else was on Freddie's list and it wouldn't have surprised her if he'd given a fortune to her mother. But Mrs Dawson did not figure in Freddie's bequests.

'He is also prepared to hand over one half of his income. Every year. Or one hundred thousand pounds in lieu. And that,' Mr Tweedie said, looking up at her, 'is a very generous offer. My advice is to take the latter. The lifespan of these pop-stars is undeterminable. It is a precarious career and may well lose its momentum.' Mr Tweedie seemed to have said it all in one breath, and Annie panted on his behalf.

'I don't want a penny from him,' she said. 'I'll take the house. I half paid for it anyway. But I don't want his money. Money, if you have it, is the easiest thing to give. It assuages a guilty con- science. I'll not let him off the hook that easily.' She meant what she said, but she also meant that she didn't want Freddie to think badly of her. Clemmie would have hit her if she'd heard.

'I think you're making a big mistake, Mrs Morgan,' Mr Tweedie said. 'You could fall ill and be unable to work. It would be unwise to say no to a nest-egg.'

Mr Tweedie was beginning to get on her nerves. 'I've made up my mind,' she said. 'And you can tell him so.'

'Would you like some time to think it over? I strongly advise you to do so, Mrs Morgan.'

She wished he'd stop calling her by that name. It didn't belong to her any more. She was Annie Dawson now, and ever more would be so. She got up from her chair. 'What now?' she asked.

'I'll go ahead with the papers,' he said. 'If that's really what you want.'

'That's what I want,' she said. She shook his hand. 'Thanks for the drink,' she said. 'I'll wait to hear from you.'

He shrugged his shoulders. 'Don't say I didn't warn you,' he said. He reached for the bottle, then put it down. He would wait for her to leave. A mad woman, he thought. Freddie Morgan was a lucky man.

Clemmie arrived early at the hospice. Earlier than was her wont. The nurse had told her to wait in reception until the doctors had finished their rounds. Another woman was waiting there, and in the silence and sadness of the place, it seemed imperative that they should try conversation. It was the woman who made the first move.

'D'you have a relative here?' she asked.

'No,' Clemmie said. 'A very close friend. And you?'

'My sister,' she said. 'Georgina. Georgie, we call her. Georgie Withers.'

Clemmie had never associated Mrs Withers with a Christian name. Let alone something as outlandish as Georgina. Her Christian name, as far as she and Annie were concerned, was Mrs. It was how the woman was forever announcing herself. 'And how is Mrs Withers?' she asked her.

'Fine,' she said. 'Just fine. We hope to bring her home at the end of the week.'

Self-deception clearly ran in the family, Clemmie thought, unless by 'bringing her home' her sister failed to add 'in a box'. For she had heard from Matron that Mrs Withers was on her way out, but was optimistically taking her time. 'Give her our best wishes. Tell her from Clemmie and Annie. Annie's my friend. Your sister knows us both.'

There was now little else to say. There were endless platitudes, of course, concerning life and death, which must have boringly echoed from the reception walls and Clemmie hoped that Mrs Withers' sister would not mention life's rich tapestry or the wages of sin. Soon a nurse appeared and told them that they could visit. The women walked together down the corridor, then parted halfway.

'It's not easy, is it?' Clemmie said.

'We manage,' Mrs Withers' sister said, saying nothing at all.

Annie was awake, smiling her greeting.

'Has the doctor been?' Clemmie asked.

'Yes. Just routine. He's kind. And silent. I like that.'

Clemmie sat by the bed and held Annie's hand. She expected the usual morning question. What's the news outside? And as usual she had prepared the answer. But this morning the question was not forthcoming. The news outside could in no way influence her state. And sadly Annie had lost her curiosity. But unasked or not, Clemmie insisted on telling her the news, wanting so desperately to keep Annie's curiosity alive. 'There's been terrible flooding in Bangladesh,' she said. 'Hundreds dead and thousands homeless.' She was beginning to sound like Mrs Withers.

Annie smiled.

'I know what you're thinking,' Clemmie said. Then both of them together, 'Mrs Withers.'

'How is she, by the way?' Annie asked.

'Fine, it seems. I met her sister in reception and that's what she told me.' She was simply reporting what she had heard. Annie did not need to know of the words unheard or the spaces between those words, the dying words, the funeral words, the farewells.

'Any other news?' Annie felt obliged to ask.

'Mr Tweedie died,' Clemmie said. 'You remember him? He was an alcoholic, the papers said. He had a drink problem was how they put it. Anyway, whatever they call it, it was the death of him.'

Annie was saddened by the news. She had not seen him again after their meeting, and her last sight of him was his reaching for the bottle and waiting for her to leave. All those divorces, she thought. No wonder he took to drink. There was no more news to report and both women welcomed the silence. Clemmie guessed how Annie was using that silence. She was on her backward travels. She hoped that she would find a place where she had been happy. But that had to be a very long time ago. Freddie time, and surely by now she had travelled that road. It was true that Annie was indeed looking for a happy place but she had found them all in her travels. So she would settle simply for moments of joy. Freddie's first touch at the club, the way he brushed her arm; his declared love under the oak tree; their first dance together; her sharing his success. Moments only, and accumulated, they thrilled her ageing body exactly as they had in her youth. She was smiling the while, and again Clemmie wished that her friend was close, smilingly close to her end. She dreaded that she would die in mourning and longing for Mary. Clemmie had called on her and had done her best.

'She doesn't want to see me,' Mary had said. 'She's made that clear over and over again. Anyway, she's earned her misery.'

Clemmie could have killed her. 'She's your mother,' was all that she could say. She thought she saw Mary falter.

'I'll think about it,' she said.

But she said nothing of this to Annie, and she dreaded that Annie might mention Mary's name. And out of Clemmie's thought, Annie spoke.

'I'm thinking of Mary,' she said. 'And kindly too.' That was all. She hoped that Clemmie would convey her change of heart.

Then she fell asleep again, and slowly a smile creased her face. Clemmie was satisfied. If Mary was in her thoughts, she might well be contemplating forgiveness. She tiptoed out of the room, and on her way down the corridor, she met again with Mrs Withers' sister.

'How d'you find her today?' Clemmie asked.

'A little tired. But she's so looking forward to going home. That's where we're all going,' she added, 'in the end.'

It was all over the papers of course. FREDDIE MORGAN MARRIES BUNNY GIRL was the gist of most of the headlines. There was a picture of them both, confetti-showered, outside the Town Hall. Happy, handsome, and heart-breaking. Annie took to her bed for a week. She rarely ate and hardly slept. The phone didn't stop ringing, so she took it off the hook. Only Clemmie was allowed inside the house and it was she who warded off the press who hung around the front and back doors. Annie was inconsolable, tormenting herself with reading and rereading the details of her calamity. Her name

was, unsurprisingly, Alison. Twenty-four years old. They met on
a cruise. Alison was a croupier in the ship's casino and Freddie
was listed as star performer in the cruise entertainment programme. This was for ever, Alison was quoted as saying. And a
similar platitude was voiced by Freddie. Mention was made of
his first marriage to 'one Annie Dawson'. Its phraseology
marked her as a discard, one thrown on a rubbish heap. She was
a nothing, and had presumably been a nothing for all their married life. The couple would honeymoon in Barbados and
afterwards would settle in a country estate in Hampshire.

Thus she read, and reread until one day Clemmie could stand
it no longer. And she took all the papers, now a week old, yesterday's news, a nine-day wonder, and she burnt them in the
living-room grate. 'Enough,' she said. She forced Annie out of
bed and into the shower. 'You've got to pull yourself together,'
she shouted through the shower curtain. 'I'm taking you out to
lunch and we'll talk about what to do.' Though she knew that
there was little that they *could* do. She recalled the day that
Colin had left her. It's true there'd been no publicity. None the
less, like Annie, she had taken to her bed and wished to die. And
when Annie had heard of Colin's desertion, it was she who had
forced her out of the house and helped her to get her life
together once more.

The press had given up on an Annie interview, and the drive
was once more free. Annie could safely emerge. They went to a
small neighbourhood restaurant and took a corner cubicle.
Clemmie ordered two vodkas and a bottle of wine.

'You're looking very pretty,' Clemmie said. And meant it.
Annie had taken trouble with her dressing and make-up and
Clemmie was heartened by this sign of recovery. They waited
for the food to be served. Then, 'Any plans?' Clemmie asked.

'He left me the house, you know,' Annie said. 'I'm going to sell it. Just the house. Not the annexe. He's given the annexe to Mary.'

Clemmie was astonished, but she was aware of the ambivalence of such a gift, so she made no comment.

'It's too painful to stay there on my own,' Annie said. 'I'll buy something that has nothing to do with him.'

'That's a good idea,' Clemmie said. 'Does Mary know about the annexe?' she asked.

'I suppose his solicitor must have informed her. I haven't seen her for months. Not since that terrible day. I haven't seen Milwaukee either. It's a long time not to see people living on your doorstep. I think Mary's in Oxford and Milwaukee's probably gone with her.'

'And your mother?'

'She's still around. She came over when Freddie left. Wanting the news. I'm happy not to see her. Especially now.'

'When will you put the house on the market?'

'Today,' Annie said. 'And I'll start looking seriously for something else. It'll take my mind off things. Perhaps.'

'D'you want me to come with you? See new places?'

'I could do with the company,' Annie said.

That afternoon they did the estate agent rounds. And over the next few weeks they inspected various properties. It was a depressing business. It seemed that most owners were selling for sad domestic reasons. Usually divorce or painful separation. Over the weeks Annie recognised danger signals. Spray airfresheners were the most common and were usually put into service to disguise faulty drains. Neither was she fooled by the coloured towels, flannels and soaps in the seemingly unused bathrooms. Especially the towels that seemed to have been folded with a ruler's measurement. This anal fixation disturbed her and told her much about the sitting occupants. She did not favour the aura they would leave behind. The bedrooms were the surest giveaway. Flouncy curtains, sink-into carpets, lavish bedspreads and sundry lacy pillows – all such over-stated decor was a sure indication that very little was going on in the bed. So Annie bypassed such properties, nervous of the angry ghosts that could not be bundled into a removal van.

At last she found a property that she knew would suit her. It belonged to a lady who was selling for proper and decent reasons. She had recently been widowed, and was going to Canada to live with her daughter. It was a cottage, with a lovingly tended garden, and the house bore all the signs of a long and happy partnership. It was clean, but untidy. It sported bookshelves, overladen with books. Not a sniff of air-freshener and the towels in the bathroom were unfolded. In the bedroom was a carelessly made bed, a bedside radio on a side table and a pile of books. Annie saw herself there and, for the first time since Freddie had left, her spirits rose, seeing herself able to live alone and even to be happy.

Her own house was easy to sell. Advertised as the former home of Freddie Morgan, the agent had to ration prospective buyers. And it was sold very quickly to the highest bidder. The exchange of properties was smoothly effected, and it was not until the removal van pulled up on Annie's drive that Mrs Dawson learnt that she was losing her neighbour. And leaving the removal men to get on with their job, Annie went to the annexe to visit her mother.

She was alone. The patience cards were set out on the table, but she was standing by the window, viewing the puzzling removal van.

Annie let herself in. 'Mother?' she called from the hall. She had always called her 'Mother', and often she had wondered why. Her mother never qualified for 'Mummy'. Even when Annie was a child, Mrs Dawson had insisted on that Mother title. Perhaps she thought it was posh, and spoke of manners and lineage. Or maybe that's how she viewed herself, a woman with a simple status, a status that did not entail affection.

She turned from the window. 'What's happening?' she asked, though she knew, for what was happening was very clear.

'I'm moving,' Annie said. 'I've sold the house. Just the house. The annexe belongs to Mary. Freddie has put it in her name.'

Mrs Dawson sat down, overcome with information. 'But I can still stay here?' she asked. First she had to see to her own comfort.

'Of course,' Annie said. 'Mary's unlikely to turf you out. You two are very close,' she commented. 'Where is she, by the way?'

'In Oxford of course.'

'With him?'

'By him, I suppose you mean Jimmy. Yes, Jimmy's with her. They're renting a flat.'

'Who's paying for that, I wonder.'

'Jimmy is. He's got a job.'

'That's illegal. He hasn't got a work permit. And how has he managed to extend his visa?'

'I don't know anything about that,' Mrs Dawson said. 'He's got a job. That's all I know. And they've got a flat. A very nice one. I've been there. They get on very well.'

'I'm glad to hear it,' Annie said, though she was far from glad. She felt very isolated and she resented her mother being privy to news that it was her right to know.

'Why are you moving?' Mrs Dawson asked.

'The house is too big for me now. In any case, it has bad memories. I want a clean slate.'

'A pity,' Mrs Dawson said. 'It's a lovely home.'

'It's not a home, Mother. It's a house.' She was losing patience. 'I'm unhappy there. My husband has left me. My daughter managed to break up my marriage.'

'Well,' Mrs Dawson said and there was a glint in her eye. 'Now you know what it's like.'

'What exactly does that mean?'

'Well, the apple doesn't fall far from the tree,' her mother said.

'All these riddles.' Annie was irritated. 'I don't know what you're talking about.'

'I had a daughter did exactly the same to me.' Mrs Dawson got into her stride. 'Why d'you think your father died?' she shouted. 'He died of a broken heart. That's what he died of. You killed him with your stuck-out belly. You broke my marriage, my girl. Now you're having a taste of your own medicine.'

Annie had to sit down. She couldn't believe what she had heard. She understood now, that her mother's life, since her widowhood, had been spent in pursuit of revenge. It accounted for her siding with Mary, her belief in Milwaukee, her visits to Oxford, and she even began to feel sorry for her.

'If you want to believe all that,' she said softly, 'then you'll have to learn to live with it. It has nothing to do with me.' She didn't ever want to see her mother again, but out of pity she said nothing. She left the annexe holding back her tears. She meant to rest and lean against the oak tree to stem her tears, but the oak tree was no place to pull herself together. It was, after all, the site where her marriage had first fallen apart.

She trudged back to the house, but there was nowhere inside where she could be alone. The removal men were all over the place. One of the bathrooms was empty, and she rinsed her face but her eyes were swollen and she longed for some privacy to cry herself out. She sat on the edge of the bath and set to wondering about her mother and how all those years she had nurtured such bitterness, had actually deluded herself into thinking that her daughter had killed her husband. She must have imagined that she'd had a wonderful partner, and years of happy marriage, an illusion so very far from the truth. But when did that delusion begin? Annie wondered. Had her widowhood necessitated such a fantasy or had it sprouted on the first day of her marriage? From what Annie recalled of her childhood, there had been no signs of loving in that house. She never saw them touch each other. But she did remember his barking orders and her meek obedience, neither of which could be construed as happiness. Perhaps her mother had to maintain such a pretence. It somehow made her widowhood more respectable. But once freed, the victim tends to become the bully, and that was the role that her mother was now playing. Despite her mother's accusation, Annie knew that she had not broken her father's heart. What had killed him was shame and fear of what the neighbours would think. She was able to pity him, but that was easy now because he was dead. And she had never mourned him.

The removal men were almost finished. They had left the kettle and a few mugs on the draining board in the kitchen. She went downstairs to make their tea. She was glad of their company, strangers who had nothing to do with her past, and their conversation likewise. Annie said that she would lead them to the cottage. She saw the men out of the door then slung her coat over her shoulders and left the house. She went to her car without looking back. She drove quickly down the drive, shielding her gaze from the oak tree and from the annexe, which was no longer a neighbour, and the postbox, too, and its dead letter. As she turned off into the road, she checked that the removal van was following her and she uttered a large sigh of relief that she had left it all behind. Unwarranted, she thought, for she knew that all she had left was the house. The rest, Freddie, Mary, Milwaukee and even her mother, were travelling with her.

Clemmie was waiting at the cottage, and together they unpacked and arranged the furniture. After a few hours, the cottage looked as if Annie had lived there for a long time. She was happy with the move, but the aftertaste of the annexe still soured her. She thought of telling Clemmie about her mother's outburst, but though Clemmie was her closest friend with whom she shared almost everything, the annexe episode was too private and too shameful to share. It would fester alone in her mind, while she wondered how long her mother could live with such bitterness. And if she died, would that solve anything? Her father's death had been welcomed, but he had left a legacy of disturbing memories. As with her mother, she supposed, with her bequest of bitter silence, that silence of betrayal that had sent her to Sheffield and which she had never forgotten. There was no point in wishing her mother dead. The sour annexe aftertaste, Annie realised, was in her own mouth, and no death or even an apology could sweeten it.

She enjoyed the cottage, and daily she relished its privacy. She went to her school but no longer volunteered for extra duties. She was coping well, but she was not happy. She had begun to believe that she had had her share of happiness. That had been her portion, and there were no second helpings.

One day, a short while after she had moved, she remembered that she had left some clothes at the dry cleaner's close by her old home. When driving in the area, she had avoided the house, unwilling to stir its miserable memories. But that day she could not avoid it since it lay on the same road as the dry cleaner's. It was a beautiful day, a garden-sitting day, and she slowed down as she passed the drive. From the opening, she glimpsed two figures standing against the oak tree and for a moment she saw herself and Freddie leaning there in happier times. She rubbed the illusion out of her eyes, but still they stood there, the two of them, and quietly she stopped the car. And refused to believe what she saw. She stifled an inward scream and, weeping, she stumbled the car out of sight.

O n her way to Annie's room, Clemmie saw the doctor coming towards her.

'Annie's not talking,' he said. 'I doubt if she will speak again. But you can still talk to her. She can hear you.' He put his hand on her arm. 'She seems very restless. I sense she is having a troubled sleep.'

It wasn't a sleep, but it was certainly troubled. The sight in the driveway, against the resonant oak tree, had clearly struck Annie dumb. Her eyes were closed but she wasn't sleeping. She sensed that for the rest of her allotted time, though she no longer had an idea of its span, for that time that was left to her, she would see only with the inner eye, and speak only with the inner voice. She would see nothing unless it was already in her mind and she would give voice only to herself. She felt Clemmie hold her hand and she presumed that her face had responded

with a smile. She hoped so. A smile for her long friendship and
loyalty.

'It's a terrible day,' Clemmie said. 'Raining and very cold.'
She was glad to announce such a day at such a bedside. She
would not have mentioned the sun or the warmth. Annie
squeezed her hand. She meant it to be a signal for Clemmie's
silence. She had too much to see with her inner eye, too much
to utter in her inner voice. She wanted silence to orchestrate
them both. Clemmie understood, and simply sat and watched
her. The doctor was right. Annie seemed restless and troubled.
Her face twitched and her fists outside the sheet were clenched.
Her mouth was tight, as if her jaw had been locked, as if, with
no words to release, it had become redundant.

But Annie didn't need a jaw, nor sight with open eyes. She
could see the two figures very clearly, and her scream was stifled.
She recognised Milwaukee first. Nothing surprising about that.
He had every right to lean against the tree. So had Mary by his
side. But what right did Mary have to a swollen belly, and one
that was close to ripeness? Mary's story had been true, Annie
accepted. She was about to become a grandmother to her ex-
husband's child. She should have been overjoyed with her new
status, but the child's provenance sickened her. How could she
love a child from such a source? And moreover, how could
Mary love it? And then she realised that Mary herself had had an
equally loathsome source. Yet she had loved her, and hopefully
Mary would do the same. And for the first time since his arrival,
she looked kindly upon Milwaukee. Father or not, and most
certainly not, she told herself, he would take care of her, protect
her, and help her raise a baby that had nothing to do with himself. She felt a tear drop from her unseeing eye, as she realised
that she would not live to see the child born. But she was

confused. All that was then, a long time ago. A girl it was. Shelley, Mary had called her. An American name, possibly Milwaukee's suggestion. She recalled sitting miserably in her cottage, trying to reckon when Mary would come to term. She hoped she would be given a sign. She was tempted to ring the annexe, but she was too proud. In any case, how should she have known about the belly in the first place? Nobody had informed her, though her mother had been given her telephone number. Clemmie had sneaked around the annexe looking for a sign. A pram perhaps, or a stray teddybear. But she had come up with nothing. And then one night, Annie was woken by a tearing pain in her stomach. She knew it as a sympathetic labour pain. By the morning she would be a grandmother.

All day she stayed inside the cottage, waiting for the phone to ring. Then she heard a bell, but it seemed far away. Perhaps in Matron's office. Then another ring. The lunch or breakfast bell perhaps. Or an ambulance or a fire-engine. And at last a ringing that was so close to her ear. In the cottage perhaps. But struggle as she would, she could not locate it. Her head was full of bells. But where? And when? Was it the then, when there was always a tomorrow, or the now, when there was only yesterday? Her head throbbed in the confusion. Clemmie felt a sudden grip on her hand, and a tear that tried to hide itself stole down Annie's cheek.

A gain it was all over the papers.

FREDDIE AND ALISON PART.

After only three months of marriage, the golden couple has come to the parting of the ways. Irreconcilable

differences are given for the reason of the break-up.
Neither party agreed to be interviewed. Freddie is
reported to have left the marital home in Hampshire,
where the gates are securely locked against callers.
Friends of the couple were not surprised. 'They were
always quarrelling,' one of them said. 'Alison used to
scream at him, and Freddie just walked away.'

That's made my day, Annie said to herself as she read the
morning paper. She was delighted and she felt ashamed of herself. But that did not worry her. When the phone rang, she
knew it would be Clemmie sharing her pleasure.

'Serves him right,' Clemmie said.

'Her too.' Annie's feelings for Freddie were still protective
even though he had been the cause of her dubious grandmoth-
erhood. They speculated about where Freddie had gone. And
had he found out about Mary? And was that the reason why his
marriage had suddenly soured? They decided to celebrate.
Annie would make dinner and Molly would come with the
boyfriend she had suddenly found. And a couple of colleagues
from Annie's school.

'It's time we were good to ourselves,' Annie said. And
straightaway she went out to do the shopping. It was the first
time that Annie had felt happy since Freddie had left. And she
had no scruples about its cause. She wondered whether he
would now come back to her and wondered too whether she
would accept him. What he had done was unforgivable, and his
denial even worse. But she knew that she was not strong
enough to refuse him. She knew too that he was unlikely to
return. She had begun to cope without him and to be content
with her own company. But she feared that, as time passed, she

might well become hooked on living alone, and thus become unliveable with. As Clemmie was. And Molly. For although she sported a new boyfriend, he was but the latest in a string of many. None of them had lasted very long, and she admitted to relief on being left alone.

Molly was the first to arrive with her latest acquisition. They get younger and younger, Annie thought, but Molly always had the sense to drop them in a pre-emptive move before they would walk out on her. On meeting him, Annie gave Gary a couple of months, rather less than the normal run of Molly's consorts. For he was too pretty, and too empty of conversation. She wondered when Molly would finally throw in the towel. But for the moment she seemed happy with him.

Clemmie was next to arrive, bearing wine and flowers. The longest-term loner of them all, she seemed a natural source of advice and consolation. So she was not short of friends. Nor enemies either. For those who have bared their secret woes often, in time, tend to resent those who have been privy to them. Unlike Clemmie, who blamed nobody. Not even Colin.

Then Derrick arrived, the geography master at Annie's school. With him was Brian, his partner, though he would never have introduced him as such. He behaved as if Brian was some-body he had just run into on the street, although they had lived together for over twenty years. Derrick never pleaded for gay emancipation, since he hadn't quite yet emancipated himself. They too brought wine and were full of good cheer. They had read about Freddie's fall, and presumed that this was a faintly bitching celebration, and they had come to share Annie's delight. But Freddie wasn't mentioned by anybody during the whole evening. The silence that covered his name seemed to heighten their celebration.

James was the last to arrive, smelling of the formaldehyde from the biology lab where he spent most of his teaching hours. James wasn't married. Neither was he gay. He was neutral in every respect, except when he was teaching, in which state he was in overdrive. His pupils loved him and he was popular amongst the staff. Annie had often wondered how he spent his time alone.

She looked around the table and dared to count her blessings. A good job, a lovely home, and good friends. All that had to be enough to offset a daughter who was wary of facing her, a grandchild whom she had not seen, a mother for whose appearance she had little appetite.

They talked of general matters, topics in which all guests could be included. It was distinctly different from the suppers she had given in Freddie's time, when the talk was exclusively show business and her contribution was solely cooking and serving. Yet she missed those evenings, but she could no longer protect herself with her doubts. Freddie had raped her daughter and Mary carried the proof of it. The proof that she had not been invited to view. She looked across the table, and James was smiling at her. It was as if he had noted the melancholy that she was at pains to hide and Annie gave him back a smile, knowing that he had seen right through her, and she offered him a second helping of dessert in gratitude.

Gary had been silent most of the evening. Yet he didn't look bored. Rather he looked embarrassed. Once or twice he had tried to offer an opinion, encouraged by Molly, but each time he lost confidence and dried.

'Come on, come on,' James urged him. But Gary didn't need encouragement. He needed a hole in the floor. Annie helped him to more pudding.

The guests stayed late, and when they had gone, Clemmie insisted on helping with the clearing-up. It had been a good evening, the women decided, a breakthrough in a way. Yet Annie was oddly depressed. The presence of company had accentuated her loneliness. Most of the evening she had managed to put her grandchild out of her mind but now she could think of nothing else. The thought of the child's father blunted her appetite to see the baby, but the thought of her daughter as its mother cancelled out its seedy provenance. She was tempted to ask for an audience, because that would be the nature of her request. Her last meeting with Mary, when she had divulged the rape, was anything but friendly. She had virtually called her a liar and it was unlikely that Mary would welcome her. Moreover, Annie was proud.

'In time,' Clemmie said, 'Mary will be in touch with you. I'm sure of that. We just have to be patient.' She included herself in the waiting and Annie was comforted a little.

But weeks passed, and she heard from nobody. She had stopped hoping for Freddie's return yet she still followed his career in showbiz papers. She knew he was in London fulfilling a recording contract and that gave him less excuse to ignore her. She had to accept the truth that she was not likely to see him again.

But meanwhile, dear James from biology had begun to court her. He had clearly never approached a woman before and he was callow in his advances. Occasionally Annie agreed to be taken out for supper. But with little pleasure. The break-up of her marriage had so shattered her that she believed herself to be untouchable, unwantable, and that any man who found her otherwise was lacking in good taste. As a result she grew to dislike men as a class, to hold them in contempt and derision. She regretted this attitude in herself and she wondered whether she would ever overcome it. Thus poor James, who had once been a friendly work colleague, now became a target for her ridicule, and shortly he withdrew from the contest, believing himself to be an inept wooer, and he retreated to the safety of his laboratory. Nevertheless, he was determined to try again. But not too soon.

Annie coped, and she tried to tell herself that that in itself was a triumph. But she knew that she was only half living, as if zombied into mere coping. 'Pull yourself together,' she said every morning to her reflection in the bathroom mirror, but there were too many distraught parts of her to assemble.

It was a Saturday. Supermarket day and Annie picked out a trolley far too large to accommodate her needs. But a small basket would have matched her single status and of that she was ashamed. She perforce had to gather provisions that validated her choice of carriage, collecting far more food than she could consume alone. She did the same every Saturday, and short of the odd supper-party, most of the food went to waste; that food she was really buying for Freddie, for Mary, for her mother, and now the new baby. Indeed she paused at the shelf of nappies and wondered what size was required. And as she stood there she heard a young woman's voice.

'She must have had her baby, then.'

Annie turned. The woman was smiling. Mary's age. Young.

'Who?' Annie asked.

'Mary, of course. Your daughter. We met before. In Oxford when you came to visit Mary. Mary and I shared digs. I'm Imogen.'

'Of course,' Annie said. She was very nervous. She had no idea who the girl was, though her face was vaguely familiar.

'What did she have? A boy or a girl?'

Annie didn't know, but she was damned if she would show it.

'A girl,' she guessed and she hoped that she was not asked for the name.

'You missed a lovely wedding,' the girl went on. 'Mary said you were away.'

Annie trembled. Whose wedding? she thought, and she felt her knees melting. But how could she ask?

It seemed that they were blocking the gangway with their over-the-trolley gossip, and they had to manoeuvre themselves out of the way. Thus there was a pause in their conversation, which gave Annie time to either escape or face the information that she knew was not good news.

'Were there many there? At the wedding?' Annie invited what she sensed would not be good for her.

'No. Just a handful. Jimmy wanted it quiet. So did Mary.'

Jimmy? Annie thought. The name of a stranger.

The girl was gabbling on. 'He's lovely,' she was saying. 'Potty about her. They'll make a fine pair. They say American men make great husbands.'

Then Annie's knees *did* give way and she gripped the trolley to prevent herself from falling. She hoped her near-collapse was not noticeable, and she was glad when the girl said, 'Must rush. Give my love to Mary,' and swept her trolley down the aisle.

Annie looked for somewhere she could sit down. At the end of the store there was a bench for weary shoppers. But she was not weary. She was simply devastated, and she needed to compact her body on to a solid seat, else she feared it would dissolve. For the penny had only just dropped. Jimmy Winer was the name, her daughter's so-called father. Mary had married Milwaukee.

*

Clemmie watched as yet another tear stole down Annie's cheek and she wondered whether she would wipe them both away. She knew that Annie wasn't sleeping, but whatever she was doing, she didn't want to disturb her. It would not be long now, she thought. Annie had already overstayed the doctor's prognosis. By almost two weeks. Perhaps God, or whoever was in charge of things, was being generous and allowing Annie time to complete her circle of recall.

Inside her mind, now so pulsating, so active, Annie was acutely aware of time, aware of the deadline, and she knew that she could no longer indulge in flashback. That there was no point in recalling, for instance, her impetuous marriage to James of biology. James, who, so hooked on living alone, fled between meals to his laboratory, and finally, to Annie's relief, didn't come home. No point either in recalling her promotion to headmistress. Or Buckingham Palace where the Queen awarded her the OBE for services to education. Useless, too, to recall Molly's final rejection of men and her loving partnership with an actress. No point in recapping any of these. None was pertinent to Milwaukee.

No. Chronology was now imperative. Mary has married Milwaukee. What now? She's sitting on the bench in the supermarket, trying to look tired, too weary to move and make space for a genuinely weary customer. She needs the space to herself. Space to hold herself together. She thinks of the baby and concludes that Mary's marriage does not mean that the baby isn't Freddie's. Perhaps Milwaukee loves Mary enough to be its stepfather. But supposing, despite the truck, despite the tattoo, despite the phantom walks in the parks, he was *indeed* Mary's father, as Mary so believed, what in God's name was she doing marrying him? Annie writhes on the bench. She doesn't think she can make it back to the cottage. James's sudden appearance is a godsend. Precious time taken out of his laboratory for quick Saturday shopping. He carries a basket. He sees that she is breaking and he asks no questions. He helps her up from the bench and practically carries her to his car. He settles her in the cottage and still no word has passed between them. Until he leaves.

'Call me whenever you want,' he says.

She lies on her bed and craves sleep. A tear falls from her eye.

Clemmie wiped it away along with the others. She squeezed her friend's hand and thought she might offer up a prayer. But she decided against it. She had too little faith.

That night Annie spent burying her pride, and the following day she drove to the annexe. She had a key but she refrained from using it. She was a caller. No more. Her mother answered the door.

'I wasn't expecting to see you again,' was her cold welcome. She made no move to ask her inside.

'I hear Mary's had a baby,' Annie said. 'I'd like to see it.'

'She's out. They've gone to Oxford.'

'Is it a girl, then?'

'Yes. Shelley.' She still did not ask Annie inside.

'Who's the father?' Annie dared to ask.

'You of all people should know that. Mary already told you, and apples don't fall far from the tree. But you wouldn't believe her.'

'She'll find it hard to get a husband now,' Annie said, testing how much her mother knew.

'You found one easy enough,' Mrs Dawson said bitterly. 'Mary might be lucky too.'

So she didn't know about the marriage, Annie concluded, though she might well be covering up. She decided to say nothing.

'Tell Mary I called,' she challenged, thus putting the ball squarely in her daughter's court. 'You have my telephone number.'

Mrs Dawson shut the door and Annie went back to the cottage and waited for the phone to ring. But it didn't, and after a week she decided to write to Freddie. She sent the letter care of his agent, and her address and telephone number were clear. She wrote that Mary had given birth to a daughter and perhaps he might be interested in seeing his child. In effect she was telling him that there was no longer any doubt in her mind that Mary's rape story had been true. Nevertheless, she sent him her best wishes. She hesitated before posting it. She was aware that her letter ruled out any possibility of his return. But she no longer craved for that. Since the birth of the baby, she was growing to hate him.

She received a reply almost by return of post.

Your letter only confirms the reason why I left you. You no longer trusted me. You were no longer loyal. I wish Mary well enough, but I have no desire to see her baby. The child has nothing to do with me.

He didn't send her his best wishes, or even kind regards. He simply signed his name.

When she had left their old house, she had discarded everything that reminded her of Freddie. Except for his letters. Those she took with her in their be-ribboned bundle. Letters from all over the world. His touring world. Stories of his concerts, of backstage events, clippings of his rave reviews, and always with the rider of how much he loved and missed her. Now she went to her bedroom and took them out of her drawer. Since moving into the cottage, she had not as yet lit a fire in the quaint Victorian grate. She could think of no better way to baptise it. She lit a little kindling on the grille. Her sacrifice merited a fine conflagration. She lit the sprigs of wood and listened to their hymn-like crackle. And she watched the letters burn. Occasionally she deciphered a phrase of love, but she felt no pain. Instead she was flooded with relief in the knowledge that a chapter that she had been so loath to close was now for ever sealed. She did not regret what she had done. But that night she dreamt of Freddie and longed for him.

She had shared the news of Mary's marriage with Clemmie, who found it hard to believe. There were so many questions that had to be answered, but there was no one to approach for replies. Mary was clearly not available and, presumably, neither was Milwaukee, and Mrs Dawson's lips were viciously sealed.

Then Clemmie suggested a private detective. It seemed the only way. He would have to be told the full story, the possible lies and the possible truths.

'But what exactly do we want to know?' Annie asked. And then, as a wise afterthought, 'What exactly can we afford to know?'

'Everything.' Clemmie said. 'Who is the baby's father? Who is Mary's father? Who is Milwaukee? We want the truth. Whatever it is, you have to be prepared for it. We'll find someone,' she concluded, 'and I'll come with you.'

It was left to Clemmie to find a reliable and confidential

sleuth. Within the week, she came up with a name, highly recommended, she said, though she couldn't divulge her source of recommendation. Clemmie was behaving like a gumshoe herself. They set up an appointment with a Mr Feather early the following week. A five o'clock appointment after Annie's school.

Clemmie met her outside Mr Feather's office. It took a while to recognise her, for Annie was wearing a blond wig.

Clemmie laughed out loud. 'Nobody's investigating you, Annie,' she said. 'You're in the clear.'

'I don't want anybody to know what I'm doing,' Annie explained. 'If anyone, say, who knows Mary or my mother saw me going into this office, they'd put two and two together and send out warnings.'

Annie had a point, Clemmie conceded. Besides, she looked good as a blonde.

Mr Feather did not keep them waiting. They were ushered straightaway into his office. He was smartly dressed, though in old-fashioned style. His trousers sported turn-ups, and there were cuffs on his jacket. He wore a waistcoat and, instead of a tie, a silk flowered cravat. As he moved to take his seat, Annie noticed that his shoes were clad in spats.

Though as yet he knew nothing of the case, Mr Feather seemed eager and ready to go to work, and although Annie warmed to him, she suspected that he had very few cases on file.

'Would either of you ladies wish for coffee?' he asked. He had an old-worldly manner which matched his appearance, and both seemed totally at odds with his calling, one that must occasionally involve underhand and sleazy manoeuvring. But Clemmie and Annie accepted his coffee offer for both were wary and in favour of delay. They exchanged weather pleasantries until the coffee came and, after the first sip, Mr Feather said, 'Now, tell me everything you know.' He pulled his pad towards him and extracted a gold fountain-pen from his breast pocket. Clemmie nodded to Annie, giving her the floor.

Annie did not know where to begin. She herself did not know how it had all started. She knew *where* it had started, and when, but she didn't want to mention the truck. She would tell it without frills, just the facts of it and hope that Mr Feather would not notice or question the omissions. She confessed to Milwaukee, and explained his name, then his desertion and Mary's birth. She did not mention her mother's silence, or Aunt Cassie or Uncle Will. Neither did she describe her father's funeral. He died, was all that she said, with no mention of her relief. She dispensed with her marriage and divorce in one breathless sentence. Then Mary's quest for her father, the discovery of his name and her journey to Milwaukee. Then quickly to Milwaukee's appearance and how she considered him a fraud. Then the accusation of rape. And, finally, Mary's pregnancy and her marriage to Milwaukee. Then she took a large gulp of coffee, considering her job done.

Mr Feather, too, paused for breath on Annie's behalf, and so did Clemmie, who, despite knowing the story, detail by detail, could make no sense of Annie's précis.

'I sense that there is a lot that you haven't told me,' Mr Feather said kindly. 'I will need many more details. Let's go over it again, shall we, and you won't mind, I hope, if I interrupt you occasionally to make a point clear. Let's start with this Milwaukee fellow,' he said.

And so Annie was obliged to repeat her story, while Mr Feather made unhurried notes with his elegant pen. To give him adequate time, Annie was often obliged to pause in her narration, which gave her time to ponder on the omissions of her original account. Moreover, there were pauses for Mr Feather's questions, which forced her into overall honesty. As a result, she found herself confessing to the truck, the details of her marriage and divorce, her father's death, and her mother's bitterness. She left nothing out, and her confessions gave her a modicum of relief.

It took time for it all to be done to Mr Feather's satisfaction. He smiled at the women and opined that they deserved a further cup of coffee. He poured it from the silver pot on the tray and delicately handed them the tongs for the cubes of sugar.

'I'll do all that I can for you,' he said. 'Some areas of the investigation are straightforward, others require much research and perhaps intrigue. As I said, I'll do my very best. It's not an uninteresting case and I look forward to it.'

Annie felt he was thanking them for giving him something to live for, and she hoped that his best was going to be good enough.

He took them to his door, and bowed them out. It would not have been out of character had he kissed their hands and Annie found herself wondering how such a civilised sleuth could hang around under lamp-posts, or climb up to bedroom windows to photograph proof of adultery. And, at the same time, keep his spats spotless.

They decided to treat themselves to lunch. In the car on the way to the restaurant, Annie discarded her wig. 'Remind me to wear it when Feather's around,' she told Clemmie. 'Otherwise he'll start investigating me.'

They laughed together. They were both relieved by the confession.

As they turned into the restaurant car-park, Clemmie saw

them first. And she tried to engage Annie in conversation so that they could pass by unnoticed. But Annie saw them through the rear window. Unmistakable. Mary and Milwaukee, pushing the pram between them. She stopped the car suddenly, so that she could stare at them as they passed. She made to get out, but Clemmie stopped her.

'Be patient,' she said. 'This is not the time.'

Annie knew she was right. The urge to have a first view of her grand-daughter was painfully compelling and she had to hold on to her seat until she was sure that they were out of sight.

'Well done,' Clemmie said, squeezing her arm.

Annie parked the car, having lost all appetite for food. 'I can't eat,' she said.

'What you need is a drink,' Clemmie said. 'I'll have an orange juice, then I'll drive you home.'

But Annie had started to cry and Clemmie had started to be stern.

'You have to be strong,' she said. 'I know it's not easy for you. I know it's heart-breaking. But you'll see Mary soon enough. And the baby. I *know* it and you have to believe it too.'

Annie sent the tears back where they came from. She needed to be alone, to let them free.

And they do. Back in her coma. She knows that a coma is always in the present. It's too late for the past, and pointless for the future. She lets the tears flow. And Clemmie sat by and watched.

Where does Mr Feather start? the tears ask. Does he go to

Oxford? Does he even go to Milwaukee? Is he bent on an incest trail? What can he do that I can't do? Except ask the questions. See the baby. Kill Milwaukee. Yes. He started it all with his hoaxing. And before him, her mother with her cock-and-bull Major. And before her, her father, who'd sent her from home. And before him, the belt that would not buckle. And before that, the truck. And before that, there was no before. She is in danger of flashback, and she knows there is no time for that. It is in the now that she must deal with Milwaukee. She must kill him. There's no other way. She drags him into the back of the truck. Any old truck will do. She sits on him and spits into his face. Then she takes his arm and marks the spot where the tattoo should have been, and she stipples it with her needle, slowly, painfully, and, mindful of the art and in immaculate inlay, she fashions a bird. He is writhing, begging for mercy, but she has not finished. With disgust, she takes a rag and lifts his member. She does not slice it off. Too quick. Too painless. She saws it slowly, and with infinite relish. He is silent, appalled, and beyond pleading. No point any more. He has lost his *raison d'être*, which he should never have had in the first place. His face is distorted with the pain and she watches him with pleasure. 'Go back to Milwaukee,' she says to him, 'and try your luck there.' She thinks of killing him, there and then, but that would be too generous. Let him do it himself, if he has a mind to. Or let him live a man-less and women-less life in misery. She spits on him once more.

Clemmie watched Annie's hands as they beat the sheets with uncommon strength. And her face had reddened with rage. Give her time, Oh God, she prayed. She is so far away from for-giveness.

*

Hardly a week had passed before Mr Feather telephoned Annie and asked her to come and see him. 'A little progress,' he said, his voice smiling. 'I look forward to seeing you.'

She insisted on taking Clemmie with her. Clemmie knew the right questions to ask and, unlike Annie, she was not burdened with the need to be thought well of.

Mr Feather welcomed them. The coffee tray was already on his table.

'Just a little to report,' he said. 'I have checked the birth information of the child. It was born two months ago at the Radcliffe Infirmary in Oxford. It weighed six pounds and nine ounces. It is registered in the name of Shelley. Its mother is Mary Dawson, and the father is registered . . .' He looked up at the women, knowing that that was the information they were waiting for. They knew that Mary was the mother, that the child was a girl and its name, and its weight and site of birth was information hardly worth paying for. They waited for Mr Feather to divulge what they had come for. Or at least part of it.

'The father is registered as "unknown",' Mr Feather said. Then after a pause, 'What d'you make of that?' he asked.

'She knows all right,' Annie said. That 'unknown' sounded like a woman who was promiscuous. 'My Mary's not like that,' she said and wondered whether she knew her daughter at all.

'So you think she's covering up for someone,' Mr Feather said.

'I'm sure of it. But why?'

'That's my next move,' he said.

'What are you going to do?' Annie asked.

'I have to think about it,' he said. He sensed Annie's disappointment in his performance. 'It's early days,' he added. 'There was one other thing. I don't know how I forgot it. The marriage. That is valid and legal. The register shows that one Mary Dawson was married to one James Winer three months ago. That is shortly before the baby was born. His occupation is given as carpenter.'

Annie sniffed with contempt. In her mind Milwaukee's only full-time occupation was as a sponger, which would hardly look well on a marriage certificate.

'But she swears he's her father,' Annie said.

'And that's my next move.' Mr Feather rose. 'I'll be in touch with you as soon as I have more information.' He saw them to the door with the same courtesy as before. Mr Feather would not be ruffled. 'It's a question of patience,' he said. 'I'll be in touch shortly.'

But it was almost three weeks before Mr Feather contacted Annie once more. Again she took Clemmie to his office. He seemed more dapper than before. Almost chirpy. He wore the same old-fashioned suit, but his cravat was less demure. It was multi-coloured and garish. It looked as if it called for a hippie slogan. A large half-eaten hamburger lay on his desk. Mr Feather looked as if he'd been to America.

Which he had, as he informed them jauntily. To Milwaukee.

Clemmie mentally totted up the expense account that was not included in his services. She hoped that the journey had been worthwhile.

And as if Mr Feather read her thoughts. 'It was well worth the trip,' he said, 'though the city itself is very dull. What a pity your Milwaukee didn't live in New York,' he chuckled.

The women laughed politely.

'It was well worth it,' he said. 'And you'll never guess who I met.'

Annie was slightly irritated by his manner. She hadn't come to his office to play games. 'You tell *us*,' she said shortly.

'I met with your Milwaukee's brother.' He paused for applause.

'He has a brother?' Clemmie asked.

'Not only that,' Mr Feather smiled. 'That brother is a mine of information. I didn't tell him who I really was, of course. I told him I was a soldier in the British Army. I made myself a private, though between you and me, I rose to the rank of Major. I told him I'd made friends with his brother in London and we'd spent a bit of time together. We'd corresponded for a bit, and he told me that if I ever hit Milwaukee to visit him. Well, I've hit it, I told his brother. We were such good friends. I laid it on a bit. I told him I thought it would be a real gas to see him again.'

It was clear that Mr Feather greatly enjoyed his job, and Annie felt that his pleasure might have blunted his efficiency. She wondered how Milwaukee's brother could be of any help in the investigation. And Mr Feather was about to tell her.

'First of all,' he said, taking a sip of his coffee, 'your daughter's so-called husband is already married. Yes. I checked. He's married all right. With three children. Never got a divorce. Pays no maintenance. The law have been after him. So has his wife. It's no wonder he took the chance of getting away.'

This was indeed news and in itself worth the trip, Annie thought. 'So we can report him,' she said, 'and the marriage can be annulled.'

'And as a result of bigamy,' Mr Feather said gleefully, 'he can be deported. So that gets rid of your Milwaukee. Just leave it to me.'

'Wait,' Annie said. 'Don't be so hasty.' She was thinking of

Mary. Suppose Mary was deeply in love with this man. Really adored him. What kind of mother was she to tear that love apart. Illegal as it might be, she could not invite the law to her side. It was up to Mary to discover his deception, and as long as she loved him, she hoped she never would. 'No, Mr Feather,' she said. 'I don't want you to do that. Not yet anyway. His being deported doesn't really solve anything. Does nothing except perhaps break Mary's heart. It's more important to discover the baby's paternity. And Mary's for that matter. If he really believed he was her father, how could he let her marry him?'

Mr Feather was clearly displeased. He thought he'd made an excellent start. He'd expected a measure of appreciation.

Clemmie sensed his disappointment. 'But at least we've got something to go on,' she said, 'even if we don't act on it immediately.'

'Was that all you could get out of his brother?' Annie asked. She suspected that there was much more, and perhaps Mr Feather was angling for another trip to Milwaukee even though he thought it a boring city.

'All I could get at the time,' Mr Feather said, 'but I suspected that there was more that he could divulge. I think he was worried about loyalty. Listen,' he said, leaning forward across his desk, 'he's a poor man. He rents just one room with a bit of a kitchen. It's pretty shabby and he's unemployed. Not married. No girlfriend. I think he would welcome some cash. Then loyalty wouldn't be a problem. But I didn't want to offer him money without consulting you first.'

Annie looked at Clemmie. Neither was wavering about the money but both were wondering whether they'd chosen the right investigator.

'Perhaps you would like a moment to discuss it,' Mr Feather suggested, and he rose from his chair and left the room.

'We can't pull out now,' Clemmie said. 'I know I'm not paying, but I'm ready to trust him.'

'He did discover bigamy,' Annie said. 'I suppose that's a plus. Anyway, we don't have any alternative.'

She went to the door and signalled that they were ready.

'We want you to go ahead, Mr Feather,' she said.

'You've made the right decision. I'll be off to the States tomorrow.'

He clearly had no other cases on his file. He showed them to the door with his usual courtesy. 'Have a nice day,' he said.

A month passed and there was no word from him. Annie rang the office only to be told that he was out of the country and it was not known when he was coming back. Annie feared that he had emigrated, taking her fat advance cheque with him. Perhaps he was not in Milwaukee at all, but in New York, which he preferred. Perhaps he had never been to Milwaukee in the first place and had made up the bigamy story to cover his tracks. Since Freddie had left her, she had fallen into the habit of trusting nobody, and she disliked this trait in herself, for it limited her capacity for friendship. She comforted herself with the thought of Clemmie, whom she could trust totally.

But Clemmie too was worried by Mr Feather's silence, although she could not bring herself to mistrust him. Perhaps he'd had an accident, or was ill, and was lying in an American hospital that was delaying treatment until paid in advance. But she did not put this suggestion to Annie. Her friend was not short of money, and she was generous to a fault.

She decided to go to Mr Feather's office herself. Perhaps he was hiding there. But on arrival, his secretary seemed no wiser than she was. She had heard no word from him, she said. And she too was worried. He never failed to keep in touch. But she didn't want to involve the police. Or the missing persons bureau. She was in favour of waiting.

'How long?' Clemmie asked.

'Let's give it another week,' she said.

As Clemmie turned to leave, the main office door opened. She saw the spats first, or rather the spat, and she was tempted to embrace him.

But Mr Feather was unembraceable. Only one foot was shod and spatted. The other spat merely protected a plaster cast that reached to his knee. His face was bruised and one cheek was alarmingly swollen. The women rushed to help him into his office.

'I'll make some tea,' the secretary said, as if a cuppa would make him all better.

He sank himself into an armchair and attempted a smile. 'Mugged,' he said. He considered that that explained everything. 'In Chicago. On my way to the airport. Two weeks in hospital. I'm better now.' He tried another smile.

If he was better now, Clemmie wondered, what must he have looked like when they first picked him up? 'You should go home and rest,' she said. 'Forget work for a while. You're not fit for sleuthing.' Then she smiled too.

'There's work to do,' he said, 'and some I can do from my desk. Tell your friend I have lots of news. It's rather disgusting, I'm afraid, but it does shed a little light on the case in question. Tell her to come tomorrow.'

'No, I won't,' Clemmie said. 'All that can wait. I'm going to take you home after you've had your cup of tea.'

He smiled at her, grateful. 'I've a taxi outside,' he said. 'I just wanted to pick up some papers.'

'Those can wait too,' Clemmie said. 'Now drink your tea and be on your way.'

As she left him, he said, 'Have a nice day.' Then, 'No, I didn't mean that at all. That's what the man said to me after the mugging. I was on the floor, but I heard him quite distinctly.'

Clemmie reported the news to Annie, who sent Mr Feather a box of chocolates and instructions not to return to the office until he was mended. She was impatient for his news, and curious about what he called its disgusting content. Nothing would surprise her about Milwaukee. She just hoped that Mary was not part of that scene.

C lemmie had not moved from Annie's side for two whole days and nights. She had watched the silent pantomime of her musings, sometimes calm and peaceful, but more often restless and raging. And she held her hand all the while. She needed to stand, to walk around, to breathe fresh air. Once or twice during the night, she had left the room, fearful of the risk she was taking, for she did not want Annie to die alone. Each time she left the bedside, she had to loosen Annie's hand. But Annie still kept her grip intact, though it clasped nothing except the coded imprint of Clemmie's hand. When Clemmie returned to the bedside, that hand was fluttering in panic. Clemmie held it in her own. Annie groaned and turned her head sharply to one side. She sees Mr Feather minding his own business, walking down the entrance that leads to the airport. A hand grips him from behind, while another, also from behind, relieves him of his briefcase and wallet. He thinks they've got all they want. Now they'll leave him alone. He makes no move to defend

himself and this annoys them. He deprives them of their high.
For the money, or whatever, is only secondary. It's the kicks they
want, the punches, the blood and the broken skin. So they floor
him. Horizontal, he sees people walking by, rushing to the
check-in. Some pause, look and hurry on. Mr Feather hears a
crack in his leg, feels a blow to his cheek, smells blood, turns his
head and sees four feet running behind him. Have a nice day,
they tap out. Have a nice day. 'Oh,' he says. And 'Oh,' again. A
crowd gathers round him and stares. Just stares. A spectacle. He
closes his eyes on their indifference. Mary, he whispers. Then,
Milwaukee. He has a tale to tell. It will keep. Patience. Patience.

The following week, Mr Feather rang Annie to tell her he was
ready to see her. According to Clemmie's description of his
wounds, she had expected to wait much longer and she sensed
that his impatience to tell his story had got the better of him.

Clemmie was surprised at his improved appearance. His face
was almost back to normal. He was still in plaster, though it was
a smaller one, which covered his foot and ankle. He wore the
same old-fashioned suit, with a modest silk cravat. Both spats
were back where they belonged. He was chirpy, eager to pro-
ceed. But first he insisted on coffee, and the ceremony of the
sugar-tongs and the creamer. And he had to sip at it first before
sorting his papers on the table.

'I went to see his brother again. Joe, that's his name. Short
for Joseph, I suppose. He was surprised to see me. And suspicious. I expected that and I knew I had to come clean. I
confessed that I had never met his brother, that I was an investigator and that I needed information. He was silent. Perhaps he

was struggling with notions of loyalty. I'm prepared to pay, I told him. It didn't take much to overcome his scruples. He owes me, he said. How much? It depends on what you can tell me. I don't come cheap, he says. I need the money. Look how I live, he says, as if his penury were my fault. I do what I can to help my poor sister-in-law. Jimmy left her nothing. He scratched his head as if he were adjusting a halo. Poor Maybelline, he says, which I presume is the name of Milwaukee's discard. I offered him a hundred dollars. That's just for starters? he says. It depends what you tell me. Oh, I can help you plenty, he says, but it'll cost. What d'you want to know? I want to know, I said, how your brother met Mary and what happened between them. You're in luck, he says. He told me everything. He held out his hand and I obliged him with another hundred. I hoped that that would be enough.'

At this point in his narration, Mr Feather felt the need for more coffee. Also the need to add suspense to his tale, for he knew that the best part was to come. Annie and Clemmie accepted the coffee he poured for them, then the creamer and the tongs. But they were impatient. They knew that Mr Feather was teasing them, but in view of his injuries and all his hard work they bore with him, and pretended to relish the coffee.

'And then?' Annie asked when she felt she'd been tolerant enough.

Mr Feather put down his coffee cup, satisfied that suspense had been served. 'He took the money,' he said 'and stuffed it together with the first hundred into the breast pocket of his shirt. Then he tapped it with satisfaction. He's not what you would call a pleasant man, our Joe.'

Annie could have done without Mr Feather's continual

commentary, but she accepted that this was his chosen style and was part of the pleasure of his work.

'Like his brother,' Clemmie put in to show that she was an appreciative audience.

'Exactly,' Mr Feather said, smiling at her. 'Tell me all you know, I said to him. Like I told you, we were close, he said. Jimmy told me everything. About Maybelline, his marriage, his kids. He'd left her and he was living here, renting the room next door. That's how I was here when Mary came. He asked her inside, into my room because it was bigger and tidier. I hated to think what Milwaukee's room looked like if it was even worse than Joe's.'

Again Mr Feather threatened commentary. 'I can't tell you what a mess that room was in.'

Annie waited for him to itemise the mess and Mr Feather obliged.

'The kitchen, if you could call it that, was on a shelf. A dirty kettle and a gas-ring and a rusty ice-box. The waste bin was overflowing. The bed hadn't been made, the sheets were filthy and the duvet as well. There was a sort of wardrobe and the door was hanging open. But there were no clothes inside. Instead there was a range of coloured rubber sheets hanging there. I wondered about that.'

Annie prepared herself for his speculations.

'Seemed rather perverse to me,' Mr Feather mused. 'Perverted almost. I have to tell you, I found no pleasure in talking to that man.'

Clemmie commiserated, and Annie felt that she was enjoying the suspense and she hoped that she would not encourage it. She was irritated. She had not paid out good money, and there seemed to be no limit on it, to have Mr Feather investigate coloured rubber sheets and dig out the sordid story that must lay behind them. All it proved was that Milwaukee came from a very poor stock indeed, but she had sensed that on first meeting him, without having to spend a penny. She was beginning to lose her patience. 'What happened then?' she asked. 'You say Mary came into his room,' she reminded him in case, with his opinions, he had lost his thread.

'I know where I am,' Mr Feather said, faintly offended by her allusion to possible loss of memory. 'Mary came into his room, he said. With his brother and she poured out this story of him being her father. She told him how she had found him, then about her mother and her stepfather and how famous he was. We pretended to have heard of him. We noticed that she was very well dressed and she looked rich. Then when she suggested that he go back to England with her and meet her mother, all expenses paid, I noticed that Jimmy began to get very interested. He asked her if she would give him a minute to think things over, and he dragged me into his room to talk about it. The first thing he said was that she was quite a dish. He obviously fancied her. And he has a way with women, does my brother. He's handsome. No question of that. I sensed what he had in mind. A free trip to England, a good life. If only he could pull off the scam. But most of all, it was a God-given opportunity to get out of the country where he was wanted for more than just not paying maintenance.'

'More?' Annie asked.

'I pressed him for the "more",' Mr Feather said, 'and I was not surprised when he again held out his hand. I gave him fifty this time, and he seemed satisfied. The bill joined the others in his shirt pocket. It was bulging by this time and I was wondering where he'd stash the rest of my greasing, for I was sure that wasn't the end of it. What more was he wanted for? I asked him. Theft, he said. Wife-battering. But they had no real evidence, so they left him alone. But he was always frightened of being caught. A free flight to England was exactly what the doctor ordered. Those were his very words,' Mr Feather said.

Annie waited for the commentary, but this time it was not forthcoming. Mr Feather stuck to his tale.

'So we decided, Joe said, that we'd go along with it. Why not, he asked me. I might even scrounge enough to get you out of here too. England's not a bad place. Then we went back into my room. My brother put on some act, I can tell you. He'd only been in London one night, and he'd gone to the dance but left to go to the pub instead. But he welcomed that girl as if she was really his long-lost child. He held her in his arms and wouldn't let her go, winking at me over her shoulder while he did so. He had to get a passport, he told her. And some clothes, and she pulled out a wad of notes and gave them to him. She said she would book him into her hotel and they'd stay there together till he was able to leave. She was over the moon with happiness and I felt very sorry for her. Jimmy told her to go back to her hotel. First he had things to settle and then he would follow her. When she was gone, he gave me instructions. I had to find out about her stepfather, get his recordings, so that he could claim to be a fan. And to find out about parks in London where he would have taken Annie for walks. Then he went off to the hotel. I'll see you right, Joey, he said. Well, nothing came of that, did it? I'm still here in this hole, and he's never sent me a penny. So he owes me.'

Mr Feather leant back in his chair and, as Annie expected, he poured himself more coffee. Which gave her time to reflect on the information he had gathered. It sounded genuine enough.

It had come from the horse's mouth, or at least his groom's, and it served to confirm what she already suspected. She was saddened by her daughter's gullibility. 'Did he tell you anything else?' she asked.

'Yes. Quite a bit more. And the most interesting part.'

Mr Feather was teasing again, and Annie felt she ought to offer him a bribe to continue, in the same way as he had greased Joe.

Mr Feather sipped his coffee, and Clemmie grew impatient.

'Do get on with it, Mr Feather,' she begged.

'You want to know the rest,' he said. 'And so did I, believe me, and when I asked Joe to go on, he put out his hand again. What I haven't told you is really worth something. Worth a fortune, I'm telling you. I hesitated. I knew I had to give him something. I couldn't risk not hearing the worth that he promised. I offered him twenty-five, but he shook his head. Worth more than that, he said. I gave him the same as before but his hand still stretched out on the table. Then I took a risk. I rose from my seat and I said, I think you've taken enough. Don't be in such a hurry, he said. Sit down. Take it or leave it, I said. He wasn't happy, but he agreed.' Mr Feather paused. 'D'you know,' he said, 'I think – it's just occurred to me – he might well have been the man who mugged me. It's possible, don't you think?'

Annie waited for his musings.

'He knew I was leaving that evening,' Mr Feather went on. He could have driven to Chicago with a friend. Makes sense, doesn't it? Still, there's nothing I can do about it, is there?' He smiled. 'Yes,' he said. 'I think it's more than possible.'

'What happened then?' Clemmie placed him back on track.

'Well, Joe said,' Mr Feather obliged, 'I didn't see Jimmy for almost a week and I didn't hear from him, then suddenly he turns up at the apartment and I hardly recognised him. His smell, for starters. Perfume, aftershave. That sort of thing. And his clothes. From the best man's store in Milwaukee. He was jaunty too, and flashed a wad of notes like he'd won the lottery. He had a lot to tell me, he said, and he took me out to dinner. And I'll never forget it, because that's the only treat I got from the whole business. Because after he left I never heard a word from him. Yes, he owes me. Sure thing. He didn't eat much. Drank a bit. He was excited. What's going on? I ask him. You'll never believe it, he says. Then he tells me what happened. I can't say I was pleased for him. Bit disgusted really.'

Annie shifted in her chair. Suddenly she wanted to go home. She was frightened of what Mr Feather might further reveal.

Mr Feather noted her nervousness. 'Can I suggest, Mrs Morgan,' he said, 'that you leave us? I will tell your friend all that you need to know. Of course you can stay, if you wish, but you might find what I have to reveal very painful.'

Annie was glad of the release. She knew about 'painful' and she knew where to go to take the pain away.

Clemmie's affectionate hand-hold anchors her in her sleep. Or half-sleep. Or no sleep at all. She has heard the doctor mention 'coma' but whatever it is called, it is comfortable, and she welcomes it. It ignites recall. And of the most recent kind. Clemmie reports from Mr Feather. Painful, she says. But she doesn't mind. Not here. Not in her painless coma. She sees the restaurant. Vegetarian. Up-market. No smoking. Expensive, tasteless, monumentally dull, Milwaukee in full flow, high on his story. His brother gapes. She's quite a dish, Milwaukee says. She asks me to her room. I flirt with her a bit. Hugs and things. Not too much though, because I'm supposed to be her dad. But then she kind of responds, but a bit more than she should if she thinks she is my daughter. She has the hots for me, that Mary. No doubt about it. I don't know what to do, because I have the hots for her too. So we play round a bit, me the dad, and she my kid, then she drags me over to the bed and I think that both of us are villains, but which one of us is going to confess first. I don't have to worry because she says, I know you're not my dad. You're just pretending to be. All for a free flight to England and a place to live. And all the time she's saying this, she's unbuttoning my shirt and my trousers and that's a relief so I don't have to be her dad any more. And I tell you, she's some lay, that Mary. Been around quite a bit. That's all they do in Oxford, she says. Then we rest a bit, and do it again. I think I love her, Joe. It's real this time. We've got a plan.

Clemmie watched as Annie writhes on the bed. She pressed the bell at the bedside, and straightaway a nurse entered, the morphine angel.

My Mary's not like that, Annie screams inside herself. Then is calmed and wonders why. They have a plan, Milwaukee says. They're going to London. Mary's going to pass me off as her dad. But why? Joe says. Why can't you just go as a couple? I think Mary wants to get back at her mother. They don't get on. But the morphine is working so Annie is not upset. Bemused rather. She sees a pattern of compelling repetition in the Dawson female line, and she thinks of her mother whom she has already forgiven, and she smiles.

Clemmie squeezed her hand and prayed for her end. And for a farewell smile that would soften her own loss.

*

Mr Feather had done his job well, although he had uncovered unpleasant facts that were difficult to accept. But Annie was relieved that he would not have to go to Milwaukee again. Mr Feather had by now fully recovered. His investigation had satisfied all her requests, even the one that had concerned her most: the identity of Shelley's father. In the light of what Mr Feather had revealed, she was now pretty sure that it was not Freddie. If, as Joe had pointed out, Mary had done the Oxford rounds, then it could indeed have been anybody. That was the theory that Mr Feather proposed, and did so delicately, for he respected Annie and wouldn't have wished such a daughter on her. Annie was overcome with remorse that she had doubted Freddie, angry at herself for her own lack of trust. She could not help but admit that she deserved to lose him.

'I don't see what more I can do,' Mr Feather was saying. 'The 'father unknown' declaration on the birth certificate shows quite clearly that Mary, even if she does know, will keep her mouth shut. That leaves Milwaukee. Maybe he can be bribed like his brother, but it's possible he doesn't know either. I suggest, Mrs Morgan, that you learn to live with it, painful as it may be. You can still love the child. She is, after all, your own flesh and blood.'

And who else's? Annie was forced to wonder. And anyway, what did Mr Feather know of Freddie and her marriage that might have been needlessly broken. And what, moreover, did he know of Mary who didn't want to see her, let alone show off her child. But all that she couldn't confide in Mr Feather. It would in no way help his investigation. He was virtually telling her that his services were no longer required. He offered her some more coffee, but suddenly she was deeply depressed by the coffee

ritual, the silverness of it all, and she rose to leave. Clemmie followed her example.

'You've been very helpful,' Annie told him. 'I shall expect
your account,' she said. She wanted to put the transaction on a
purely business level. She had begun to resent the necessary
invasions into her privacy.

As usual Mr Feather ushered them out with courtesy and
Clemmie sensed that he was relieved to see the back of them.

'What now?' Annie asked in the car.

'It's a cul-de-sac, I'm afraid,' Clemmie said. 'Mr Feather's
right. There's nothing more he can do. It's up to us now, but
I've no idea where we should start. You have to wait for Mary
to come to you and then, perhaps, you can have a heart-to-
heart. She'll come, I'm sure. You just have to be patient.'

Annie agreed. But she had no intention of being patient. She
could be dead before Mary came around. Somehow or other,
she had to initiate a meeting. And if not with Mary, then her
mother would do for starters. She needed to know what part
she had played in the conspiracy. Did she know of the wedding?
And above all, did she know of the baby's father? But her last
visit to the annexe had been an unpleasant one and it was
doubtful that her mother would let her inside. So that left Mary.
But how?

It happened by chance. Not with Mary, nor her mother. But
with Milwaukee.

She had gone to give a talk to a new school that had opened
in the suburbs. She had had lunch with the newly appointed
staff, and on her way home she noticed that she was low on
petrol. She pulled up at the first service station on her way. She
filled up the tank and went to pay. As she entered the service
station she saw that there were two servers at the counter and

one of them was Milwaukee. Clearly legit. He had married an English woman and had received a work permit thereby. But Milwaukee saw her too, and clearly hoped he'd seen her first, for he dodged into the back of the shop. There was a small queue at the counter, but Annie didn't join it. She would wait for Milwaukee's return. She waited while the queue grew longer and the man at the counter was obliged to call his colleague back. He didn't appear at once. He was clearly allowing time for Annie to pay and leave. Meanwhile the queue grew longer and the man at the counter grew testy. He couldn't leave the counter untended. There were bound to be thieves around.

He called his name. 'Henry,' he shouted, 'you're needed.'

Henry? Annie thought, but was not surprised. Milwaukee was a man of many parts and each part, no doubt, had a different handle. She wondered what poor Maybelline called him.

At last 'Henry' was obliged to put in an appearance and Annie duly joined the queue. He saw her and his Henry face fell. There was now no escape. She stared at him, but he avoided her gaze. He dreaded her approach and when it came it was his turn to serve her.

She put her money on the counter and said, 'I need to talk to you.'

'Not here,' he said.

'Yes,' Annie whispered. 'Here and now. We could go outside.'

'I can't,' he said.

'Then in that case, Jimmy Winer, I'll talk to you here and I'll not be lowering my voice.'

He trembled and waited to have a desperate word in his workmate's ear. The workmate was not impressed.

'You'll have to wait,' he said. 'I can't manage this lot on my own.'

'You heard him,' Milwaukee turned to Annie.

'Pity,' Annie said. 'Then it'll have to be here. At the counter. Loud and clear.'

Milwaukee was quick to leave his post. His workmate stared at him, furious, with a report to the manager and a sacking buzzing in his head. Milwaukee had fled and he was cowering outside against the air-pump. He'd not been prepared for such an encounter. Mary had convinced him that they were not likely to run into her mother. Which was why he had taken a job in the suburbs to avoid her. He didn't know how much she knew, so he could not prepare himself. He heard her walking towards him. He dared not look up. He felt cornered.

'Jimmy Winer,' she called. Then she stood in front of him. 'Look at me,' she shouted.

He raised his head.

'I hear you married my daughter,' she said.

He didn't answer but he knew there was no point in denying it.

Annie did not mention bigamy. She would save that for later. It might prove to be a trump card.

'Don't you find it odd that a father should marry his daughter? I would have thought that is against the law. At least in England it is.'

'I'm not her father,' Milwaukee had to own. 'I never was.'

'I knew that,' Annie said. 'I knew that from the start. Why did you do it?' she asked.

'It was Mary's idea,' he said.

What a fine husband he must make, Annie thought, so quick to lay the blame on his wife. 'Why would she want to do that?' she asked.

'I think she wanted her own back.'

'Whatever for?'

'Well, you know you don't get on too well, the two of you.'

Annie deeply resented the comments of a stranger on her relationship with her daughter. 'What have I done that she should want revenge? Tell me. You seem to know all the facts.'

He straightened up. There was no point in cowering. He would try belligerence. 'She wanted to trace her father.' His voice was threatening. 'And you,' he said with contempt, 'you didn't even know his name. You'd cooked up some cockamamie story about some major. Some hero or other, with medals. She grew up believing that she was the daughter of a hero, and she spread it over the school. She was so proud. She told me she used to look at his photograph and cry. And suddenly, out of the blue, he doesn't exist any more, 'cos he never was. Then she asks about her real father. Why didn't you have the guts to say it was a truck? She was right. You're a slut. How d'you think she feels, saddled with a mother like you?'

Annie raised her hand and slapped him squarely across his face. Her wedding ring, which she had never discarded, caught his nostril and she was glad to see the blood flow. He raised his arm to reciprocate, then thought better of it.

'You lay one dirty finger on me,' Annie said, 'and I'll call the police.' Then she turned and left him. She hadn't mentioned the baby. That would have to wait for another time. She was trembling as she sat in the car. She felt dirty, as dirty as Milwaukee had implied. But she hated him, this false revenant, and she hoped to God that Milwaukee, whoever and wherever he was, was good and truly dead.

*

She was anxious to get back to the cottage, to sit alone in its silence, to temper her anger and achieve some calm in which to consider her next move. Once there, she sat quietly at the kitchen table, and considered abandoning all plans and letting Mary get on with her deceptive life, her mother too, so that she might be freed to get on with her own. But when the telephone rang, she still hoped it might be Mary with an invitation to visit, a chance to see the baby, and to view her daughter as a mother. She took her time before answering, trying to fashion her responses. But nothing took shape. She was confused enough even to hope that it wasn't Mary on the other end of the line. But it could be Clemmie. It could even, she dared to hope, it could even be Freddie. But it was a woman's voice, one with an ageing voice.

'Annie?' the voice said. 'It's your Auntie Cassie . . .'

Annie was overjoyed to hear her voice, which immediately evoked those happy months in Sheffield. They had met only a few times since Mary's birth. She and Will had come to Annie's wedding, and Freddie had warmed to them. And occasionally, when Freddie had a gig in the area, he had stayed with them in Sheffield. But there had been no contact since Milwaukee. Aunt Cassie did not even know that Freddie had left her. She was not a newspaper reader. Neither did she know of Mary's baby.

'Aunt Cassie,' Annie said, 'how wonderful to hear your voice.'

'It's sad news, I'm afraid,' Cassie said. 'Will died yesterday. In his sleep.'

Sad indeed, Annie thought. Lovable Uncle Will, with his peasant manners and appalling grammar. And who'd always been so kind and understanding.

'The funeral is on Wednesday,' Aunt Cassie said.

'I'll be there,' Annie said straightaway. 'I'll come today. Oh, Aunt Cassie, I'm so sorry.'

Although she was saddened by the news, it afforded Annie some relief, for it forced her to leave the site of all her problems, to take her mind off the doubts and uncertainties that nagged at her. Aunt Cassie's grief was real, and founded on an event of which there was no doubt, and she would take part in that event with Aunt Cassie, and mourn its reality.

She packed a small case and made for the station. As the train approached Sheffield, she recalled her first visit to that town, with her buckle-belt discarded, and her heart full of fear. And Aunt Cassie on the platform and her embrace. She looked out of the window as the train pulled into the station and half expected to see Cassie waiting there. And even Will, and she wished for those days again, the days before Freddie, before Mary even, so that Milwaukee could never have happened. But nobody was waiting for her on the platform and, on the ride to Cassie's house, she thought of Will, and of Cassie's heart-breaking loss, and thoughts of Mary, Freddie and Milwaukee were rudely brushed aside.

Cassie opened the door and hugged her for a long while. Once inside, Annie asked if she could see Will.

'He's not here,' Cassie said. 'He's in the funeral parlour. The nurses came and dolled him up and I told them to take him away. He didn't look like the Will I knew, the Will I'd lived with for so long. I didn't want to remember him looking so respectable.' Then she laughed a little, and so did Annie. Respectable was a word Will would have scoffed at.

They went into the kitchen and Cassie prepared tea. The table was already strewn with food from friends and neighbours and crates of beer for the wake that Will would have wanted.

Annie looked around. Nothing had changed in the kitchen since the time she had brought Mary in her belly into hiding. The kitchen was the largest room in the house, and everything took place in there. And in the corner still, after twenty years, the unfinished cradle that Will had prepared for Mary before Mr Dawson's funeral had dragged them all out of Sheffield. Just another way he had of spoiling her happiness. Yet she was still glad that he was dead, and only wished that he had died much sooner.

'There was nothing wrong with him,' Cassie was saying. 'He was still asleep when I got up. At least, I thought so. I came down here to make his cup of tea, and then I took it upstairs, I couldn't wake him up. I kept trying, though I knew he'd gone. I called the doctor and he said Will had been dead for at least six hours. His heart had given up on him. I couldn't understand it. I'd been sleeping by his side all night. And I'm a light sleeper. And he couldn't have made a sound. Or a movement. Bless him, he didn't want to disturb me.' She started to cry then. 'I'll miss him so,' she said.

Annie envied her a little, that she could mourn without guilt, guilt that would prolong her grief. Because they had spent so many happy years together. Blameless years. Friendship years. She could have only happy memories.

'I'm glad you came,' Cassie said.

'So am I.'

For the next few days, the two man-less women made arrangements for Will's funeral, and during that time, Annie told Cassie all that had happened since Milwaukee. The conspiracy, the rape accusation, Freddie's desertion, the marriage of Mary to her so-called father, and now the baby with father unknown. All that information was ample and shocking enough to take Cassie's mind off her present troubles. She found it hard to assimilate it all. She was saddened most by Freddie's desertion, and Annie's unhappiness. 'Will was very fond of him,' she said. 'But I don't believe Mary's story. I'm sorry, Annie, but I think Mary's a liar. Freddie would never have behaved like that.'

Then Annie was ashamed. She wished she had Cassie's certainty.

'I doubted him,' she confessed. 'That's why he left. He didn't trust me any more. But it's not to do with Freddie,' she protested. 'It's Mary. I haven't seen her for months, and she's keeping the baby well away. I know it's a girl, and I keep wondering whether she looks like Freddie. Oh, Aunt Cassie, what shall I do?'

'Nothing,' Cassie answered straightaway. 'And that's the hardest thing of all to do. You have to be patient. Mary will visit and bring the baby. And what does it matter, after all, who the baby looks like? It will look like itself, as Mary did, if you remember, and whatever she looks like, she will be your daughter's child. Your grand-daughter.'

It all made sense, Annie thought. But such logic could not overcome her doubts.

'Your problem,' Cassie said, 'is not Mary. Nor even the baby. It's Freddie, isn't it? You're not over Freddie. If you were, your doubts wouldn't matter any more.'

Aunt Cassie was right. No matter how much she protested to the contrary, Annie knew that Freddie's desertion had broken her.

The funeral arrangements were complete, and on the day of burial, the sun shone brightly and soothed their sadness. The little church was full. Will had many friends who would sorely miss him. Annie thought of her father's funeral and how coldly indifferent it was. How nobody cared that he had gone, and some, relieved of blackmail and obligation, were downright satisfied. Will would be truly missed, and often referred to over the years with affection and laughter. On his behalf, and on her own, Cassie would be cared for and, in time, she would adjust. Annie was almost envious of her status. Aunt Cassie was a widow. Respectable. Whereas an aura of suspicion clung to a desertee who had no status at all. For a moment she wished that Freddie had died, but her heart leapt at such a thought. She took it back immediately. As long as Freddie was alive, there was always the possibility of his return and she berated herself for her stubborn hopes.

The wake was solemn, and its participants sober. No one was in a hurry to leave the house, and over the next few days they visited constantly. Until Cassie suggested that she wished to be alone for a while. She wanted the house empty, so that Will's absence was no longer deniable. She even suggested that Annie return to London and get on with her life, as she proposed to do with hers. They parted in deep affection for each other, and Cassie promised that soon she would come to London and stay a while.

On the journey home, Annie considered Aunt Cassie's advice, and she knew that despite its common sense, she could not act upon it. She thought about Freddie, and if Mary's story was true, she hoped she could forgive him. And if Mary were a liar, as Aunt Cassie had suggested, she hoped that she could forgive herself. But the notion of forgiveness was untimely. Premature and ill-placed. She had to return to that place where all that was left to her was forgiveness, and its time was irrevocably ripe.

*

Clemmie's hand was steadfast and comforted them both. She stroked Annie's forehead and found it cool. Wherever her friend was, it was in a peaceful place. And she was right.

Annie is in Aunt Cassie's kitchen, that room that does for everything. She goes to the cradle that stands in the corner. Unfinished. But it rocks. Unsteadily for it needs a stabiliser. As she rocks, she sings a lullaby to Mary, who should have lain there if Annie's father hadn't decided to die and spoil everything. Well, almost everything, for in the end he's well rid of. No forgiveness in that quarter. Annie hums her lullaby and she wonders how such a delicate melody can orchestrate such malice. Yet she goes on singing to that baby who has broken her heart, for forgiveness towards her is still hopefully possible. Had Will finished the cradle it would have been for Mary, and down the line it would have been for Shelley. Then the cradle rocks violently, as if offended, and though not on any tree-top, it falls. On the kitchen floor, its frame is shredded into matchsticks. And Cassie says, 'What does it matter? The baby isn't hurt. The baby is whole.' Aunt Cassie doesn't need to be forgiven. She has never done anything wrong. Sheffield is a happy time, with its card games, and knees-ups and lemonade. Recall takes only seconds. So why does it take so long to die? First forgive, she hears Aunt Cassie say. Then you can go.

Annie's encounter with Milwaukee at the service station had shaken her and she feared what would become of it. Mary's anger, for certain. She would notice his swollen lip, and he'd be happy to tell her how he came by it. And she was bound to

come to the cottage, bursting with fury, but at least Annie
would see her. She dared to hope that she would bring Shelley
with her. But she was frightened. She needed protection. She
needed a witness. She needed Clemmie. But Clemmie was in
Brighton with her god-daughter Bonnie, and would be for a
whole week. She would have to face Mary on her own. If Mary
would come at all, she would lose no time. She would not wait
for the swelling to subside. She would hold it in her mind's eye
to feed her rage. Annie waited in fear for the knock on the
door. When it came, later that evening, she hesitated before
opening. The thought crossed her mind to pretend to be out.
But the lights were on in the cottage and her car was outside the
door. Still she hesitated as the knocking grew more persistent,
and in fear that it would wake her gentle neighbours, Annie
rushed to the door. She nursed her own anger, and surely she
was entitled to it. Mary burst inside.

'Come in,' Annie said, as Mary settled herself on a kitchen
chair.

'What in God's name d'you think you're doing?' Mary
shouted. 'Me and Jimmy are not your business.'

For a moment Annie wondered who Jimmy was. There was
no real name attached to Milwaukee. It was a place. No more.
It did not merit any further identity.

'You broke his lip,' Mary said. 'He can hardly talk.'

Now she knew who Jimmy was and she could not help smiling.

'You think it's funny?' Mary yelled.

'Would you like a cup of tea?' Annie asked. For some reason
she felt she was holding all the cards.

Her invitation angered Mary even more. 'I didn't come for a
lousy cup of tea,' she said. 'I've come to tell you to mind your

own rotten business. And don't you dare interfere with us again.'

'Well, now that you've said your piece, you can go,' Annie said. 'Back to your husband. Though I was under the impression that, according to you, this Jimmy person is your father.'

'You can think what you like,' Mary said, because she had to say something. She had to leave those unasked questions in the air. She didn't want to be confronted about anything, least of all by her mother. 'Nothing is your business any more,' she said.

'I'm your mother,' Annie reminded her.

'Some mother,' Mary snapped. 'You bring me up on some cock-and-bull story about my father. A war hero. Buried in France, you said. You even had a phoney picture of him. Some poor bugger you found in a second-hand photograph album. But when I told you I wanted to visit his grave, you're suddenly very quiet. There's no hero any more. The unknown soldier he was, but with no grave. Then when I insist on knowing who he is, and where, you can't tell me. Because you never knew his name. Some mother.'

Then it was Annie who wanted her to go. The reminder of the truck was too painful. She went to the front door and opened it. Mary passed across her, and neither said a word.

When she had gone, Annie went to the window that over-looked the street. She watched Mary as she opened the car door, and by the light of the streetlamp overhead, she saw a carry-cot inside, and she watched as Mary stretched over and fiddled with a blanket. And she saw her smile. She stayed at the window long after the car had disappeared, trying to under-stand Mary's cruelty. Had she been such a terrible mother to merit such treatment from her daughter? All she had done – or not done – was to ask the GI his name. She had done it for her own sake, for her seventeen-year-old schoolgirl sake, because she simply didn't want to know. And by the time the buckle-belt had surrendered, she wasn't even curious. She couldn't afford curiosity. Knowing who he was would not have re-buckled her belt. All she remembered was the truck, and it was that truck that she considered was Mary's father. She didn't deserve such treatment. It simply wasn't fair. She did not want to dislike Mary, though she suspected that a little dislike would ease her, would enable her better to bear her cruelty. So she concentrated on disliking her daughter a little and found it offensively easy. She would hang on to it, she decided, for her own defence. Though she knew that by the morning it would have waned.

Despite Mr Feather and all his findings, his one omission seemed to label him as a total failure. The absence of the name of Shelley's father on the birth certificate confirmed that omission. 'Father unknown'. It was exactly as she herself had registered Mary's birth over twenty years ago. At the time, the war-hero had not yet been invented. But she had told the truth. There was no more unknown than Mary's father. Could it have been a similar truth in Mary's declaration? Was it possible that she really did not know the name of Shelley's father? Was it possible that he was a truck too? A truck in Oxford? Or could it really have been Freddie and, out of kindness to her mother, she had left it undeclared. But kindness was not a trait one associated with Mary, and this gave Annie a certain hope. For if Freddie were really the father, Mary would have named him, and let others take the consequences. But it was too late now to discover Freddie's innocence. Her own doubts had sent him away. And she still was not clear of them. She had to search out the truth, once and for all. But how?

When Clemmie came back from Brighton, she could offer no
answers. She tended to agree with Aunt Cassie's opinion that
the paternity was irrelevant.

It was the Easter holiday, and Annie had no school work to
divert her. She spent much time driving around in her car, aim-
lessly. Such an occupation she found conducive to reflection,
but no ideas surfaced. She found herself driving around her old
neighbourhood. Past the house, past the annexe, and round
again. One evening, she noticed that while the main house was
brightly lit, the annexe was wholly in darkness, and she wondered whether the occupants were away. The obvious thought
of breaking-in crossed her mind. A thorough search of Mary's
belongings. Her papers, her notebooks and, with luck, a diary.
But it was risky. They might merely have gone out for the
evening. Shelley and all. But she could not pass up a possible
avenue of research, so she decided to make an innocent enquiry
at the main house. Her old Freddie-home.

As she pressed the central bell, she shivered with nostalgia and
a longing for the past. But one glance at the oak tree in the drive
erased that longing. A woman answered the door. Mrs Winston.
She had seen her before during the negotiations of the sale, and
she greeted Annie with a little surprise.

'I'm sorry to trouble you,' Annie said, 'but I'm trying to
contact my mother and there seems to be no one at the annexe.'

'They've gone away,' Mrs Winston said. 'The three of them
with that beautiful baby. They went last week. To Spain. I'm
keeping an eye on the place. I've got their address if you want it.'

'No,' Annie said. 'It's not that urgent. It will wait. When are
they coming back?'

'They've been gone for a week. So it's another week,' Mrs
Winston said.

Annie thanked her. She had enough information to formulate a plan. She was anxious to get away. Mrs Winston asked her if she wanted to come in for a coffee, an invitation that Annie was quick but polite to refuse. She wanted no reminders of her past happiness or her present misery. For both had begun to bewilder her.

On her way home, she decided on her next move. She still had the keys to the annexe. It would not have occurred to her mother to change the locks. She would let herself in in daylight, so that Mrs Winston would not be surprised by a light. She would ask Clemmie to come with her, she decided. She wanted support, help and a witness.

She slept well that night. She had found something to do and she looked forward to it with a certain excitement.

They arrived at the annexe mid-morning on the following day. Annie parked the car a good walking distance from the house and took the back-door access to the annexe, which led out to the back lane. No one was about, and they felt in the clear. And more so once they were in the kitchen.

'Where do we start?' Clemmie asked.

'Here. Why not?' Annie said. 'Then each room. One by one.'

'It would help if we knew what we are looking for.'

'Anything,' Annie said. 'Something we don't yet know about.'

'Like a paper bill?' Clemmie said, picking up a piece of paper from the draining board. She was not happy with her snooping job, but she realised that her friend would never settle until the Freddie truth was known. Only then could her doubts be confirmed or denied. And only then would she settle to take the consequences of either. And because of those consequences, Clemmie secretly hoped that their search would prove futile.

Between them they covered the ground floor of the annexe

by late morning. Annie had greater hopes of the bedrooms, which was why she left them till last. There were three bedrooms in all. If one of them was obviously shared, with evidence of his and hers clearly manifest, then there was no doubt that Mrs Dawson knew of the wedding and sanctioned its procedures. She opened the door to her mother's bedroom first. She didn't expect to find anything of interest inside. Nor did she. The drawers contained nothing more than what they were intended for. Neither did the wardrobe. Nothing was hidden away. There were no secrets. Her mother's life was an open book and thus tedious. Clemmie shadowed her every move, nervous of her own trespassing.

'Nothing here,' Annie said, shutting the door.

The small bedroom was next in line for inspection. It was a spare room, and apart from a single divan bed, there was nothing in it. Annie checked for traces of Milwaukee in case he was still considered a guest. But there was no sign of habitation. That left the last bedroom, on which Annie pinned her hopes and she hesitated before entering.

'What we're looking for is in here,' she said to Clemmie. 'I feel it in my nerve-ends.' She opened the door gingerly. As she did so, her fingers brushed the two garments hanging behind the door. His and hers bathrobes. So her mother knew. Further proof of that was the double bed, unmade, still with an indentation in each pillow, and two pairs, his and hers again, of discarded jeans on the floor. In the corner of the room was a cot, and beside it a changing-table. And in another corner, a desk. Annie stared at it. 'It's in there, Clemmie,' she said. 'I feel it, and I'm afraid to open it.'

'Shall we go, then?' Clemmie asked. She wanted out of the place. She feared the consequences of their findings.

'Sit down,' Annie said. 'I'll do this one on my own.'

So Clemmie sat on the bed feeling more of a trespasser. And she watched her friend and prayed that she would find nothing.

The desk sported one central drawer, with three drawers on each side of the hollow. Annie decided to search it thoroughly, and to that end she would take out each drawer in turn and sift its contents. First she took out the central drawer and laid it on the desk-top. It was surprisingly ordered and consisted of typing-paper, cards, stamps and writing equipment. Its orderliness hinted that nothing of interest would be found inside. Nevertheless, she sifted thoroughly, then replaced it, shaking her head. The next drawer was more promising, in that it was a jumble of various items that belonged to no particular category. There were a few purses containing small-change American coin. A comb and a bundle of fountain-pen refills. A box of batteries and some loose fuses. Then a bundle of letters and photographs. Annie hesitated, but on quick perusal none appeared to be in Mary's hand. She picked out just one, a large embossed card, ornately bordered and it was a thank-you for the wedding party and wishes for a bright future. Another letter said more or less the same. And another. And after half a dozen of these, Annie restored them to their bundle. Nothing new there. She knew about the wedding and she was indifferent to the joy of its celebration. But she couldn't resist the photographs. And all of them were of the wedding. The sight of Milwaukee by Mary's side, her bigamist faux-father, sickened her, and at their close-up kiss, she sniffed her distaste. Clemmie was watching her. She felt a shameful itch to see the photographs but she wanted no part of it. But when Annie offered them to her, she felt bound to take them, or it would have made clear her disapproval. She scanned them quickly, but without comment. Then handed them back.

The third drawer revealed a ledger book. It was empty apart from its first page on which attempts had been made in Mary's handwriting to itemise expenditure. But clearly she had not thought it worth her while. The next two drawers were disappointingly empty. And the fifth drawer was strangely stuffed with nappies and tissues. She felt for the last drawer with her eyes shut, and she kept them shut until she laid it on the desktop. It was by no means full, but it was promising in that it contained what appeared to be official papers. She took out the pile and laid it on the desk, and for the first time in her search, she sat down.

There were a number of letters from the Oxford University library confirming that certain books Mary had requested were now available. Another letter advised her of the service charge due on her flat and a request for prompt payment. And then she turned to the next one on the pile. Clemmie was watching her, and as she read the paper, she noted how her friend's face slowly coloured scarlet, and how a vein on her forehead threatened to burst. Then Annie let out a heart-broken scream. Clemmie rushed towards her and held her in her arms.

Annie knows that she is perspiring, but she knows too that the sweat is invisible. It is inside her, trickling through her every rotting bone, a raging moisture sponging her brain. She is dissolving and all because of a simple piece of paper. Mr Feather in all his diligent searching could never have found it. Brother Joe in Milwaukee probably didn't know about it. And, if he did, his telling would have cost. Who knows whether Milwaukee knew or not? And who cares? Annie thinks. But *I* know. And I am the only one who needs to know.

The paper flutters in her hand, already damp from her fingerprints. She reads it again. She knows it by heart. Every single word, every stop, every comma, and their loud exclamation marks, not on the paper, but on a roaring scream from her own throat. Read it again, Annie, she whispers to herself. It answers the last and the most important question. It also breaks your heart. Read it. The heading first. You don't understand it. But it stuns. Radcliffe Infirmary, Oxford. And its subtitle. It is printed on her retina with its shrieking capitals. Ante-natal Clinic. She echoes that recalled raucous sigh. She thinks that her eyes are wide open, staring in wonder at the text that follows. She rereads it slowly, word for startling word. Dear Miss Dawson. Mary. It could be no other. You are required to attend the ante-natal clinic for your first appointment on Tuesday, 4th March, at 4p.m. You are asked to bring a urine sample. Please be in touch if this time is not convenient. Signed, Petra Hawkins. Ante-natal Nurse. Over and over again, keeping her sweating fingers on the date under the heading. Then smudging her finger away. 15th February. And thinking back, checking and re-checking dates and weeping aloud into Clemmie's arms. While Clemmie reads and Annie points to the date and they both look at each other, for they know now that Mary was pregnant *before* she went to America and before Milwaukee. But above all, above all, before Freddie had visited her in Oxford. Above all, that. That. That Freddie is innocent. Always was. That now it doesn't matter who the father is. A truck perhaps. A truck in Oxford for, as her own rotten mother never tired of saying, the apple doesn't fall far from the tree. And that same voice accuses through the darkness, 'You killed my marriage, you and your belly.' And now my own daughter, with her lies, kills mine. And I shall bloody well make sure that, with the mention of bigamy, I shall kill hers.

The sweat now pours from her face, and Clemmie took a tissue and wiped it away.

They drove back from the annexe in silence. Annie's anger against Mary had subsided a little, for she blamed herself and her doubts. But those doubts would not have arisen without Mary's lie. So once again she cursed her daughter, and this time aloud so that Clemmie was relieved, for she knew that a silent Annie could not be comforted.

'Why did she have to lie?' Annie asked.

'Perhaps she really didn't know the father's name,' Clemmie said. Then she heard the sombre echoes of that suggestion.

'She could have called him Oxford,' Annie said. 'In that respect, I've been a good teacher.'

'She was angry with you,' Clemmie said. 'You fobbed her off for years with some kind of hero father, and then when she wanted to visit his grave, you had to come clean.'

'Dirty, you mean,' Annie said.

'Mary wanted revenge, and the whole Milwaukee story was part of that. I think Mary is truly in love with him,' Clemmie dared to suggest.

'And I sincerely hope so,' Annie said. 'As in love with him as I was with Freddie. Now it's Mary's turn. You talk about revenge?' Annie had raised her voice. 'Am I not entitled to it too? We're going to see Mr Feather.'

Clemmie would have preferred to let it all lie. What's done had been done and the proof of Freddie's innocence was now too tardy to bring him back. 'Let it be, Annie,' she said.

'I'll go to Mr Feather on my own,' Annie told her.

'If you're so determined, of course I'll come with you,' Clemmie said. Whatever the outcome, Annie was going to need her friendship.

As usual, Mr Feather ushered them into his office with courtesy. The coffee was ready on the table.

'I have no more news for you,' he said, 'so I presume we are meeting because you have news for me.'

Annie had no intention of showing him the Radcliffe letter. It was too intimate, and it pointed to a motive for revenge. It was Mr Feather himself who had suggested the charge of bigamy and she had wavered. Now she had only to tell him that she had come to a decision.

'I want him deported,' she said, 'and I want you to set the wheels in motion. Whatever it costs,' she added.

She will never see her grandchild, Clemmie thought, and Mary will never speak to her again. But clearly Annie had prepared herself for that eventuality.

'I don't want him to know that the instructions came from me,' Annie said. 'Is that possible?'

'I have to think about that,' Mr Feather said. 'It might be unavoidable. The proof of his bigamy was the result of my investigation and that investigation was prompted by you. If the parties concerned choose to enquire the source of such information, it will be difficult to keep your name out of it. But I'll do what I can. This is a police matter, you understand. I would have to work in conjunction with them.'

'I'll leave it to you,' Annie said.

'No regrets, no regrets,' she said to Clemmie as they drove home, for she knew of her friend's scruples. 'And I don't want to talk about it any more. I'm ready at last to get on with my life. Yes, I have regrets, but for my own mistakes. Nobody else's.'

Two weeks passed and they were back in Mr Feather's office.

'Progress report,' he told them. 'The police department in Wisconsin has been alerted by Scotland Yard. It seems that the Milwaukee police have long been chasing him for maintenance payments. This now-proved charge of bigamy will facilitate his deporting. Although they know the circumstances of the investigation, I have their assurance that you will not be involved.'

Both women were relieved.

'What happens now?' Annie asked.

'He will be arrested,' Mr Feather said, with some satisfaction. 'And he will be sent home.' Then, after a pause, 'Your daughter will need some comforting, I suspect.'

Annie wished he had not offered such an opinion. She didn't need to be told that Mary would be broken, as broken as she herself was when Freddie had left. And maybe as broken as her mother claimed to be when her rotten husband had died.

On their way home, they drove past the annexe. All the lights were on. The conspirators were at home. Very soon now, shattering their smug cosiness, the shit would hit the fan. She knew that they would not see her hand behind it, yet the scruples that Clemmie had nurtured now began to flower. But it was too late for regrets. Mary would have to live with desertion, as she had done.

Annie was glad that she would not have to witness Milwaukee's departure. But she read about it. A week later. A banner headline in the local newspaper. BIGAMIST

DEPORTED, it shrieked. They had come in the middle of the night, it seemed. Four of them, as if poor old pyjama-clad Milwaukee would have put up a fight. They'd given him time to pack his bags and there was a picture of him leaving the annexe flanked by his guards. A picture too of Mary, captioned, 'The woman who thought she was his wife', and Annie folded the paper and tore it into shreds, as if that gesture would erase the episode entirely. The fact that Mary did not know that it was her own mother who had set events in motion was no comfort to her. *Annie* knew and that was enough, and it was a secret that she hoped to take to her grave, too overwhelmed with shame to reveal it.

Except in a coma, where it will not be denied. Clemmie is squeezing her hand, but it's her mind that needs squeezing, Annie thinks, to choke the memory of the hurt she's caused Mary to suffer. She hears her curtain drawn, and then the doctor's voice. She's a fighter, your friend, he says. Then Clemmie. She still has business to attend to. She feels the needle prick on her skin and she knows that the shame will go away, will go back all those years to where it came from. But only for a while. It is simply biding its time.

The new term had started and Annie was glad of it. Each morning Mary was her waking thought and she wondered how she was faring on her own. Clemmie had seen her in the supermarket, but each had avoided the other. The baby had not been with her, but her trolley was full of baby food. Well, at least she has a baby, Annie thought, and whosoever was its father, it would be a comfort to her, as Mary had once been to herself.

It was the lunch-hour and Annie had stayed in the staffroom to sort out a timetable for her lessons. It was quiet in the room and she looked forward to being undisturbed for a while. But there was a sudden crashing of doors and she heard an angry rushing of footsteps down the corridor. Then the staffroom door was flung open and Mary was in the room, standing over her, breathing fire.

'You did it, didn't you. You arranged it all.'

'Did what?' Annie asked. 'Arranged what?' She was playing for time. How could Mary possibly know of her involvement? She would admit nothing.

'I've had a letter from Jimmy,' Mary said. 'My husband, in case you've forgotten.'

'I thought he was your father,' Annie said, again temporising.

'D'you want to know what he wrote to me?' Mary asked.

Then Annie knew that she was cornered and that there was no escape.

'I don't want to know.' Annie sought to defend herself.

'Well, whether you want to or not, you're bloody well going to listen.'

'I would like you to go. Now,' Annie said.

Mary laughed. 'I'm not one of your pupils. I'll go when I'm good and ready. I know about your precious Mr Feather,' Mary said. 'Joe told Jimmy everything. About the bribes he gave him. About Jimmy's wife and children. But I already knew about that. Jimmy told me in Milwaukee. We just thought if we could get away we could make a life together. And we could have, because we loved each other. Well, you saw to it that we didn't, didn't you. Just because you were so bloody miserable yourself you couldn't stand anyone else's happiness.'

'And why d'you think I *was* so miserable? Why d'you think Freddie left me? How could he possibly stay when you accused him of rape?'

'That was true. I thought you ought to know. He's Shelley's father.'

Annie stood up. 'He's no more Shelley's father than I am. I don't know who her father is and I don't suppose you know either. But one thing I do know is that you were attending an ante-natal clinic in Oxford *before* your Milwaukee jaunt, *before* your Jimmy, and long before Freddie took you to dinner in Oxford. You were already pregnant when you went to America. Tell me, Mary, who *is* Shelley's father?'

'I don't know. And that's the truth. Like you, I don't even know his name. It could be Jason, Danny, Miles, and God knows who else. It doesn't matter. But at least my baby didn't begin in the back of a filthy truck like I did. She started between clean white sheets.'

'So why, in God's name, did you accuse Freddie?'

'If you want to know the reason,' Mary said, 'we thought it might be worth a try.' She laughed. 'It worked though, didn't it? He left you. And this is your revenge. I'm glad he left. I'm glad you're miserable and I hope you'll be miserable till the day you die.'

She rushed from the room as quickly as she'd entered, with her anger not a whit abated.

Annie sat down. She was trembling. Freddie had left her because her own daughter had thought it 'worth a try'. That was all. Just a throw of the dice. Just a bit of fun. Simply 'worth a try'. Now she felt less ashamed of what she had done, but saddened by the nature of what her daughter had become. She couldn't understand it. Mary had been a good child. She was prone to sudden tempers, it was true, and Annie had ascribed them bitterly to the truck. It was the nastiness that she couldn't understand. The meanness of her nature. Her selfishness, her need to hurt. Then Annie realised she could have been describing her own mother. She doubted that she would see Mary again, and she knew that she had asked for such an outcome. Yet she couldn't help thinking that now they were quits, couldn't they be friends? But it was a foolish thought. Mary would have to find happiness again before she could entertain it. And Annie wished her that with all her heart.

She should have felt relieved. Everything was now known. There were no longer any secrets. Except for Shelley's father. And about that she was not in the least bit curious. And as Shelley grew she would no doubt reveal traits that had come from Mary's clean white sheets and she hoped that they would be palatable. But Freddie's innocence afforded her no relief. She owed him a sincere apology. She knew that these days he was spending much of his time in America but a letter care of his agent would reach him. She would exonerate him, and blame herself, and she would expect no response. This she did, and though full of regrets, the writing of the letter comforted her a little.

Is it that long ago that Mary denied me? Or was it yesterday? Not yesterday because Shelley is married now, though what she looks like, I have no idea. Clemmie saw her in the church. The groom is a doctor, she says, who never saw the inside of a truck. Sometimes the apples *do* fall far from the tree, whatever my mother said. And I mean 'said', because she's dead now and she can't say it any more. I don't weep for her, in the same way as Mary won't weep for me. My time is near. I need more of it, in order to give her time to forgive me. Then she can go on living without guilt. More time. Please, please. More time.

One morning Annie received a letter from Mary. She recognised the handwriting on the envelope. It was her first communication since her staffroom encounter, that 'it might be worth a try' meeting, some years before. She tried not to be hopeful of a reconciliation, for she could think of no other reason for her letter. But the tone of Mary's note was far from conciliatory. It was curt, and cruelly to the point. It did not even address her. Mary had not known how. 'Dear Mrs Morgan' would have been too pointed, and 'Dear Mum' beyond the realms of credibility. So the address on the envelope would have to suffice. Annie read:

> I am writing this letter because I feel it is my duty to tell you that Grannie is seriously ill. She has had a heart attack and is in intensive care in the infirmary. She is not expected to survive. She has expressed no wish to see you but you may wish to see her before she dies. Hence this letter.

It was not signed. It didn't have to be. It had simply done its duty. Annie reread the letter. It had clearly been written in haste, and that was how she had read it. But it merited more than a cursory glance. Its import was momentous. And Annie did not know how she ought to be feeling. Should she be weeping? she wondered. Or should she be relieved? All that she could feel, all that she could hear, was her mother's silence that had sent her to Sheffield all those years ago. That silence which had never ceased to thunder through the years. But she did not have to wonder whether she should visit her. There was no hesitation about that, and she dragged on her coat and drove straight to the hospital. And as she was led to her mother's bed she was still wondering what she ought to be feeling. She was grateful that there was no one else at the bedside, no one else who could interfere with her unknowable feelings.

Her mother was staring at her, but Annie could read no expression in her features. Neither surprise, nor annoyance, nor welcome. Just a stare that said absolutely nothing, because there was just too much to say.

'Hello, Mother,' Annie said, and the word sounded alien, for it belonged neither to her own voice nor to Mrs Dawson's ear. But it would have to do. She dared to reach out and hold her mother's hand.

'Who told you?' she asked.

'Mary,' Annie said. 'She thought I ought to know.'

Her mother did not look at her. What she had to say seemed to be meant for the general ear, as if the whole world was being asked to forgive her. 'I've always loved you, you know,' she said to the walls.

And then Annie broke and gripped her mother's hand for at last she knew what she ought to be feeling. 'I know,' she whispered. 'I always knew.'

'Sometimes it wasn't easy.' Her mother was looking at her now and with a half-smile. 'But all the time I loved you,' she said again.

'I know,' Annie said once more, and she lifted her gently from the pillows and held her in her arms. Thus they stayed together for a while, as Annie sifted her feelings. Pity was predominant, a pity so profound that it could totally embrace forgiveness. And a certain sadness too, for a life that had so skilfully nurtured its own misery. But most of all love, a love that had lain in hesitant waiting over the years, and was at last released.

Once back in the cottage, Annie poured herself a drink. It was a toast, she thought, a toast to that belated loving.

A few days later, another note arrived from Mary. As before, it was unaddressed. Curt, cold and to the point.

Grannie died yesterday. The funeral is next Wednesday, St Andrew's Church. Two thirty.

And so, on the appointed day, with Clemmie at her side, her non-wavering support, she drove to the church. They arrived early, a good half-hour before the service was to begin. But there were already crowds of people waiting. A silent crowd, teenagers mostly, groupies, shuffling amongst themselves with the occasional suppressed giggle.

'He's here,' Clemmie said.

Annie clutched at Clemmie's hand. She had given up hope of ever seeing Freddie again, and she wondered with overwhelming affection why he had chosen to come. 'Why?' she asked Clemmie.

'It's part of his history too,' Clemmie said.

They did not get out of the car. 'Are you waiting for him, or are we hiding?' Clemmie asked.

'Neither,' Annie said. 'Let's get a seat in the church.'

They walked openly through the church door. A group of people were already seated there, and in the front pews. Annie considered them as a rent-a-crowd, since her mother had few friends.

'Let's sit at the back,' Clemmie said. She knew that Annie was entitled to a front pew, but that her status would be overlooked. So to pre-empt such a neglect, they turned towards the back of the church. And stopped in their tracks. In the back row, alone, and almost pillar-hidden in a corner seat, sat Freddie. He'd clearly avoided his fans by access through the church back door. He stood up when he saw them and smiled. Once again Annie didn't know how she ought to be feeling, but 'ought' had no part in it. Her feelings were in spite of herself. A vaulting heart-beat, a knee-melting and an overwhelming sense of loss. Her smile, too, had little to do with 'ought' as she steadied herself towards him. He patted the seats beside his own, and held out his hand. He was offering a handshake. No more. I lived with this man long enough, Annie thought. We made love and we laughed together. We were enough for each other, enough for a lifetime. Had he forgotten all those years that he could waive them with a simple handshake?

'Why have you come?' she asked him.

'Don't you remember?' he said. 'She let me clear the table. She fought against it long enough, but in the end, she accepted me. I try to remember what was good.' He stroked her cheek. 'And so must you,' he said.

She wished he hadn't touched her. She was more comfortable with the handshake. At least that gesture had shut off all avenues of hope. But the touch. That was different. It was less final, and she cursed herself for her stubborn hopes.

Other mourners were entering the chapel. Amongst them

Annie recognised Mr and Mrs Winston, who had bought her house. Then Mary arrived. Alone. She sat herself in the front pew in the midst of all that emptiness, and the chapel echoed with the groans of the empty seats and their haughty indifference. The congregation, such as it was, stood for the entry of the coffin. It bore three wreaths. One from herself, the second probably from Mary, and the third, she suspected, was from Freddie.

The vicar gave his standard funeral address, with a deft change of name and gender, and Mrs Dawson would go to the fire as if she had never been.

The rent-a-crowd was the first to leave. Then Mary, who noted the back-pew occupants on her way out and stared right through them. The non-event was over. The rent-a-crowd would repair to the annexe and wine and dine in part-payment. And the Winstons would follow them. Outside the chapel, the groupies were still waiting for Freddie's appearance, but he would back-door dodge them for decorum's sake.

Once more he held out his hand. Annie took it and he covered it with his other hand.

'I'm going away,' he said. 'I'm going to live in the States. I've been offered a film, and I'll make my home there.' He bent to kiss her cheek. 'Take care of yourself,' he said. He turned quickly, and Annie watched the back of him as the imprint of his lips singed her cheek and all her hopes dissolved.

Outside the church, the groupies were restless, and despite their location, they had begun to chant his name, as if they were waiting outside a stage-door. Annie wanted to tell them that Freddie had gone and that he would not be coming back, but her sadness was her own and she didn't want to share it. So she passed them by as they chanted softly, unprepared for rejection.

'What now?' Clemmie asked, as they sat in the car.

'We get on with life,' Annie said. In despair one resorts to platitudes, she thought. Whatever. There was nothing else to do.

'I think you need to be alone,' Clemmie said.

Annie started the car and drove Clemmie to her house. Once back in the cottage, Annie poured herself a drink. And then another. She sought oblivion for the reality was too painful to confront.

He has gone and the years have passed. And now he is dead, Clemmie tells me. He is forgiven, although he is blameless. It is my doubts that I must forgive. My mother has gone too. And pity forgave her. Floods of it. Only Mary now. My forgiveness is ready for her. It is hers that is tardy. So many years since I have seen her. Perhaps she has wrinkles now. Like mine. Sometimes I feel them with my fingers, but my skin feels smooth. I am too young to die. Shelley's face is unlined. She makes me a great-grandmother. A boy, I'm told, and all this happiness behind my back. They say that I am dying. And there are all the signs to prove that they are right. But I don't believe it. I have a sudden God-given gift of non-credulity. So I have no cause for fear. Time does not pass. It flies and I don't know where. No doubt I shall meet it when it stops, and I shall succumb to its greeting. But for now, slow down. Please. Just for a little while. Time to tell how the end began. Then the wheel can come full circle.

When Annie retired from her headship, she felt unanchored, unused and, above all, lonely. Despite her constant committee work, her charity involvements, the occasional lunch and dinner meetings, she no longer looked forward to returning to the empty cottage. She considered inviting Clemmie to share the cottage with her. Clemmie, for her part, had considered it too. She too had retired, but her job had had none of the prestige of Annie's. Consequently she served on no committees and her social life was minimal. She knew that Annie was lonely too, but neither woman, schooled in rejection, would risk the suggestion of a live-in companionship.

It took a third party. James, now retired from his biology laboratory, amicably divorced from Annie, but still a loyal friend; it took James to propose the possibility of a two-woman cottage. And so it was settled, and all faces saved. The plan worked, and worked well. Each woman knew to give the other her own space. They entertained friends and were often invited to others' houses. It seemed that at last they had achieved a companionable peace.

Until Annie lost her appetite. It wasn't sudden. It was a slow and gradual withdrawal from food. Annie refused to go to the surgery, saying that it would pass. But when it didn't, Clemmie called the doctor to the cottage. He seemed puzzled and out of his puzzlement he diagnosed a virus.

'There's a lot of it about,' he said.

Clemmie suspected that he didn't know what the 'it' was, and that the word 'virus' let him off his ignorant hook.

'Just rest,' he said. 'It will pass.'

But for the next few days Annie could barely eat at all. Moreover she was in pain. Clemmie called the doctor once more. Fortunately he was on holiday and a locum came instead. After a few questions and a swift examination, he called for an ambulance, and Annie was rushed to hospital. More questions, more probing and then an ultrascan. Clemmie prayed for gall-stones, hernia, or anything curable. And she swallowed the unsayable word. But with one look at the ultrascan, the doctors had no problem with the word. Incurable, they pronounced. But they could give her palliative care. An outline of such treatment followed but gave no promise of improvement. Two months, they said, was all that they could offer.

At Annie's insistence, Clemmie took her back to the cottage, and over the next few days she was persuaded into hospice care.

I wonder for how many years Clemmie has been holding my hand. Or how many minutes or days. I shall carry its imprint to my grave, and perhaps Clemmie will carry mine too, when I am gone. Annie listens to her words and again the echo resounds. And now, only to one word. Mary. Echo after echo from a distant shore. She listens to Clemmie's voice. 'Mary will come,' she hears. 'I saw her yesterday. She told me that she would come. Shelley too, and your great-grandchild. All of them. They will come. Don't go, Annie,' Clemmie begs. 'Stay a little while. Wait for them. They are coming. They promised.'

Annie hears the drawing of curtains. She sees nobody except through her inner eye, that vision that blurs ageing, that irons wrinkles, that blots bewilderment, erases anger, and in all their stead, paints a smile. She sees little Mary, as she is in the Freddie days, with the doll of a baby in her arms. She feels a soft bundle on her chest and she hears a chuckle. Clemmie withdraws her hand, and in its place another rests, and another and another, all as warm and as forgiving. Annie's face tingles with a smile.

Clemmie left them alone. Perhaps Mary had words to say.

Begging words for forgiveness. Words of love perhaps, hand
baggage for her mother's journey. Gently she closed the curtain
behind her.

'It's Mary, Mummy,' Annie hears, and the 'Mummy' ships
her back to the happy Freddie days. 'Shelley's with me by your
side, and Joseph too, your great-grandchild. We're all here. We
love you, all of us. It didn't always show, I know. Sometimes it
was difficult.'

Annie smiled as she recalled, syllable by syllable, her own
mother's words as she lay dying. She feels three gentle hand-
prints on her face and she lifts her hand to stroke those three
ciphers of forgiveness. Mary's, Shelley's and little Joseph's. Her
face almost shatters into smiles.

Clemmie went to sit in reception, and through the main
doors she noticed a hearse parked in the drive. Matron was
walking down the corridor.

'Taking a break, are you, Clemmie?' she asked.

'Her family is with her,' Clemmie said. Her daughter, her
grand-daughter and her great-grandson.' Three generations of
forgiveness, Clemmie thought. More than enough to ease her
friend's journey.

'You've been a good friend,' Matron told her.

Clemmie noted the past tense. Perhaps Matron only ever
spoke in that mode. Her vocation compelled it.

'I must see off the hearse,' Matron said. Then added, 'Mrs
Withers, God rest her soul.'

That throwaway piece of news lightened Clemmie's heart.
Almost to the point of joy. She hurried back to Annie's cubicle.

'You can go now, Annie dearest,' she said aloud. 'Mrs Withers
is dead. The coast is clear.'

She sat by the bed and sealed her hand on the triple farewells.

It's not too soon to count blessings, Annie decides. I have loved in my time, and I have been loved. I forgave, and I have been forgiven. She feels kisses on her forehead. A shower of petals. After so long a silence, some simple words oblige. She knows that her life is coming to its close, and her lips quiver with its pointless précis.

'Milwaukee,' she whispers. 'It's in Wisconsin.'